PECULIAR CONSEQUENCES

The LineFolk Of London: Book Two

JAY NEILL

Peculiar Consequences (Book Two of The LineFolk Of London series)

Paperback ISBN: 978-1-0681747-5-9
Ebook ISBN: 978-1-0681747-6-6

First edition 2026

Connect with the author

- TikTok – www.tiktok.com/@jay.neill5
- Instagram – www.instagram.com/jayneill.author
- Threads – www.threads.com/@jayneill.author
- BlueSky – bsky.app/profile/jayneill.com
- Facebook – www.facebook.com/jayneill.fantasyauthor
- Visit my website www.jayneill.com to join my community and access bonus content, updates, advanced reader copy programmes and more.

For all the members of the independent author community who are so generous with their time and advice

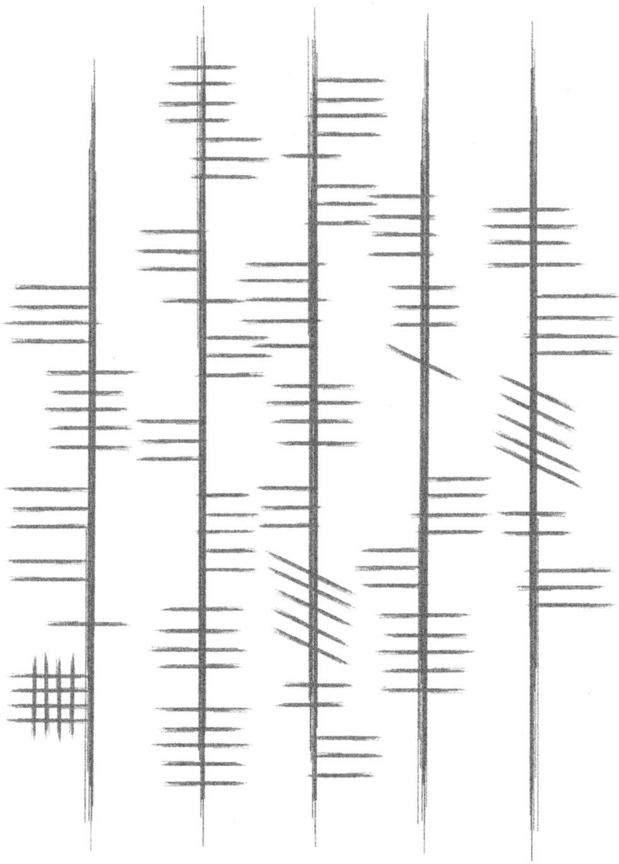

Chapter 1

Saltilack Tin Mine, Cornwall, England
March – 1852

Click, clack. Click, clack.

The sound of the chain was reassuring as it knocked rhythmically against the wooden sleepers. Every clank was a foot closer to the surface.

Ten souls, seven men and three boys, were crowded into the cart as it was hauled painstakingly up the shaft toward the tiny square of light in the distance. They had begun their journey fifty fathoms below the seabed, and five minutes after setting off from the seam at the bottom, they were at thirty fathoms, five minutes further from the gates of hell under the ground, towards what was promising to be a no-less hellish storm on the surface.

Saltilack Mine clung defiantly to the cliff edge—a Victorian engineering marvel that defied Neptune and Hades in equal measure. The tin and copper ores were inconveniently placed under the Atlantic, and only a diagonal shaft, drilled from the rugged coastline at an impossible angle, could access them. The stone buildings weathered waves, wind, and rain with little respite. Today was no different. A squall was blowing in from an ocean that had been calm when the shift descended, but was now whipped up into a frenzy that had sent the fishing boats from the nearby village scurrying for shelter.

John Puddle was sixteen. He knelt at the back of the cart in a spot where there wasn't really a seat. He had begged to take this departure rather than wait at the bottom of the shaft for the next one, because he didn't want to spend the extra hour under the ground. His widowed mother was chronically ill, and his younger sister was running the household. If he reached the surface by nightfall, there might still be time to get to the company bakery and exchange the token that made up his wages for a loaf of bread. Delay, and the purser would have shut up shop, and the family might go hungry.

The others had been grumpy about his jumping the queue, but Michael, the shift foreman, in a rare moment of kindness, had told everyone to shuffle up and make room.

"The lad's worked like Hercules hi'self today," he had said. "Let's get him home so he comes back just as strong tomorrow."

That day would come all too quickly. John hadn't seen sunlight since September. He rose from his bed in darkness every morning and was descending the shaft before dawn, only returning to the surface after the sun had set. Today was different though, and he could see a speck of brightness at the top. It was as much an incentive to get out sharpish as the prospect of bread.

Clack, clank. Clack, clunk.

The chain kept up its beat.

At the front of the cart, Elias Farmer sat holding the brake, but only lightly, the fingers of one hand brushing the handle, while he picked dust from the nails of the other. Between John and Elias, the others crouched two abreast, talking in murmurs, too tired to have an actual conversation. The youngest miner, Pip Farmer, Elias's son, was fourteen. He was in his first month in the pit and already pulling his weight like a veteran. Elias was proud as punch, and even more delighted about the extra shillings in the family coffers. Pip reached out every so often and touched the shaft walls.

"Stop that boy," said Michael Smith, the eldest at fifty-two. "Catch your hand and it will take your arm off. A one-armed man is no good to your father, or to the mine."

At the halfway point, the cadence of the clanking increased as though the mechanism at the top had realised it was hauling less chain. It was still painfully slow, but fresh air was just minutes away now.

Clack, clank, clack. Thunk, clack, clank.

John's legs were going to sleep beneath him. He adjusted his position as best he could and felt the blood returning reluctantly to his feet as needles in his soles. The cart shifted a little.

"You'll have us off the rails if you don't sit still," Michael snapped. "I'm not climbing out o'this hole. You can carry me if that happens."

"Yes, sir," John said quietly, deferring to the most experienced man among them.

"Is that the wind?" Pip asked. The shaft was usually silent apart from the chain and the flexing rivets groaning in the rails.

"Must be a nor'easter," Elias replied. "It'll be funnelling through the stack and into the headframe."

Clank, cl...

With a noise that sat somewhere between a scream and a snap, a link in the chain failed, just a few yards up the track. Whether it was a flaw in the manufacturing or weeks of pulling ore carts laden to nearly twice their limit, no one would ever know.

The upper section of the chain suddenly accelerated away as it shed thousands of pounds of load. It flicked back and forth, colliding with the shaft walls and wooden stanchions as it went. The remnant attached to the cart recoiled violently, whipping into the air and smashing catastrophically into Elias's face. He fell backward onto the shocked men and boys behind him, his grip on the brake instantly releasing, blood pouring from a wound between his eyes.

For a second the cart hovered, as though unsure if gravity was going to be its master after all, then it dropped.

The initial silence turned to screams as the passengers realised what had happened.

"The brake!" Michael shouted, scrambling over others to reach the handle.

The cart had already accelerated to a speed well beyond anything it normally achieved. The wheels bucked on the uneven rails. One of the younger men, standing in an attempt to grab a wooden beam and slow their progress, fell to the left and out of the wagon, his body smashing against the walls harder than his rib cage could withstand. He died instantly and was spared the final horror of the descent.

Michael got a finger to the brake, but it was useless against the momentum of the free-falling cart.

"God save us!" Pip cried, head down in the belly of the wagon. More bodies tossed out as it flung left and right on the tracks.

John clung to the sides, his knuckles white with the effort of retaining his seat. He watched the square of light disappear into the distance, and the sound of the wind was drowned out by the screams of men and boys.

They fell for thirty seconds and hit the seam at the bottom of the shaft at sixty miles an hour. Those still in the wagon when it suddenly stopped were crushed into each other and the unyielding stone—a chimera of limbs, metal, and rock. The miners waiting patiently at the bottom for the next cart scattered left and right as machine and human debris flew around them.

The screams echoed up the shaft long after those who had made them were dead.

At the top of the mine, the remains of the chain wound idly on its spindle.

Clack, clunk, clack.

Chapter 2

London
March – Present day

Tap, tap.

Hannah looked up from the book she was reading.

Tap, tap, tap.

"Bloody birds," she muttered and tried to settle down deeper into the sofa as if that would somehow repel the sound.

Tap. Knock. Tap.

"Axton!" she shouted. "There's a bird at the window or something. At least I hope it's a bird. The last thing that came through it was a vampire."

"The Countess is not a vampire," Mia said as she passed the doorway to the drawing room, where the nurse had taken to spending the winter evenings. "And Axton is up on the roof."

"Fine, she's a *haemovore*." Hannah took care to enunciate every syllable. "But she likes blood, and she turns into a sodding bat. And what do you mean, he's *on the roof*?"

Knock. Tap. Tappity, tap.

"Can't you hear that?" She decided it wasn't the window and glared at the fireplace instead. Maybe there was a pigeon stuck up the chimney.

"Hear what?" Mia asked, poking her head around the door, a child hanging off her arm.

"That knocking sound. Where is it coming from? Is it Axton?"

"Darling, I can't hear anything, and Ax is three stories up. If he is tapping on that window, it means he's fallen off."

"Don't you have super-cat hearing?"

"Not in this form," Mia said, looking positively shocked at the suggestion. "It's distressingly human at the moment." She touched her ears and then brushed a rogue hair back behind one before shouting up the stairs. "Ax, are you knocking something? Your colleague is hearing things."

"I'm not hearing things!" Hannah protested. "There was a tapping noise."

"Can you hear it now?"

Hannah put her finger to her lips and listened. Silence.

Mia raised her perfectly formed eyebrows as high as she could get them. She insisted werecats had nothing in common with regular tabbies, but Hannah found her mannerisms to be every bit as condescending as the moggies she had grown up with at her parents' house.

"You two are so judgmental," Hannah snapped. "I'm probably just jumpy. There's a lot to take in at the moment."

Mia leaned over and looked at the book Hannah was reading.

"Are you surprised that you are...highly strung?" she asked. "*Grundlemere's Bestiary Of Albion's Swampfolk*. That would give me nightmares, and I had a childhood friend who was a bog fairy. Once you've been on a playdate with one of those, not much else scares you."

"I want to be prepared for anything," Hannah told her. "My first couple of months here have been nothing but new and ever-more-disgusting creatures turning up on our doorstep."

"Am I disgusting to you?" Mia asked, and Hannah wasn't entirely sure if she was teasing.

"No, you are beautiful, of course, but you're a cat, and this..." She held up the bestiary for Mia to see. "...is not a cat."

"It's a gravewisp. They can be beautiful from the correct angle. Like the northern lights in miniature. And I'm not fishing for compliments."

"Perhaps you're right," Hannah said. "You had a lifetime to get on top of this. I've spent my life knowing nothing about this world until three months ago. I'll learn stuff when I learn it."

"There are wonderful things to discover, and there are some very dark things, but sitting here by candlelight every night is bound to make you a bit mad. We do have electricity, you know?"

"I like candles," Hannah protested. "But yes. More light is needed, and then I won't start hearing random tapping sounds."

Mia ushered her daughter into the bathroom next door. "Go and brush your teeth while I talk to Auntie Han." She sat down on the sofa.

"How are your scars?" Hannah asked. "Almost gone?"

"Most of them." Mia put a hand reflexively on her lower back where she had suffered the worst gashes. "There was something... dark about those things. Normally, I would have healed in days. It's been months."

"But you *are* healing," Hannah insisted. She was still learning how the therianthropic metabolism interacted with their human form. Flynn had told her that transforming between states would heal all but the worst of traditional injuries. These were not normal wounds and had lingered long after Mia had changed back to human on that night in Bloomsbury Square when Tafs died. One of the last things Wayworthy had observed before his consciousness was forever absorbed into his apprentice was that the cyoeraeths were not simply using the linether—they were creatures *of* the linether.

It was what had driven Hannah deep into the library that filled every nook and cranny of the upper floors of the abclynic. Flynn hadn't known what Wayworthy meant, but she was sure that the answer was somewhere in the thousands of books and manuscripts strewn throughout the building.

"Can't you consult him?" Hannah had asked Flynn.

"The Master's mind is not on tap!" he had protested. "It's more like entering a library with a card index and having to trawl through them all to find the correct memory."

Hannah shut the bestiary with a slap, making Mia jump. "Enough reading for tonight. I should probably sleep. I can't believe that I'm beating the kittens to bed."

"Aw, you called them kittens!" Mia exclaimed happily. "You are catching on, Nurse Chadwick."

"It's a bloody minefield," Hannah said. "When to say what. Who to say it in front of. Always on the edge of causing offence."

Mia stood up as her daughter emerged, toothpaste covering most of her face. "As you said. You learn what you need, when you need it."

She scooped the child up and headed for the upper storeys of the building.

"Mia!" Hannah called out, and her friend stopped at the bottom of the stairs. "We should talk about that night some more."

Mia smiled faintly. "I think we've discussed it enough."

"We talked about the practical stuff, sure. Moving in here. Patel organising the clean-up. What to write on the new plaque outside. We didn't talk about you, though."

"I'm fine."

"If you are, then you are a stronger person than me."

Mia ushered her daughter toward the stairs. "Go up, Trixie. I'll be with you in a moment."

"Sorry," Hannah said. "I didn't mean right now. Just that we have to look out for each other."

"Get it off your chest," Mia instructed her, a little more coldly than Hannah thought was justified.

"You lost a lot over those few weeks. Your friend. Your father."

"He's not dead." Mia put her hands on her hips, and Hannah regretted pushing the point. "You may as well have killed him, though, the way that you left him."

"I didn't have control. I just did what seemed...natural."

"It's not natural to leave a therianthrope stuck somewhere between human and animal. It's cruel. Now I still have a father, and yet I have no father. It would have been kinder to kill him properly and be done with it."

"I'm not a murderer, Mia."

"Like I am, you mean."

"No, I didn't say that." Hannah put her hands to her head in despair. "Oh, this is stupid. We all know that was a screwed-up night, and we are lucky to all be here. I'm sorry, I misjudged your mood."

"What you managed in the square was frightening, Hannah. I've never seen anything like that before; I'm not sure anyone has. If you could do that to him, you could do that to any of us."

"I'm going for a walk," Hannah said and pushed past, suddenly annoyed. "And you know what... you're really scary as well, if we're pointing fingers. "

She was halfway down the stairs before Mia spoke, her tone softer. "Hannah, be careful. It's dark out."

"I will."

When she opened the front door of the clynic, Hannah was surprised to see that there was some light in the sky. She had been lost in the book for an hour, but the city still buzzed with commuters and revellers heading for post-work drinks.

She stood on the pavement and tried to decide whether the bright lights of Oxford Circus or the tranquillity of Regent's Park were more appealing. *Park*, she thought, and set off north.

It was only recently that they had each felt brave enough to leave the clynic on their own. Patel, like most police officers, saw threats everywhere and discouraged them from taking unnecessary risks. With Mia's father, Ethelred Tarrin, now in hiding and surely nursing an enormous grudge, and given his track record of trying to harm anyone who got in his way, the detective warned Hannah in particular to stay indoors. The assumption was that he would think twice before seeking revenge against his own family, but Hannah was vulnerable to him.

None of them knew if Tafs and her brother, Dafyd, were the only two cyoeraeths in London; in fact, no one understood much of anything about these creatures. They had stepped straight from the pages of LineFolk myths, and when they were killed—Tafs by her friend Mia, who was protecting Hannah, and Dafyd by Flynn as he fought to save the linether—it looked as if the beasts had returned to the underworld.

Hannah reached for the personal alarm that Patel had given her and put her thumb over the button cover, just in case.

Tap, tap, tap.

She stopped and peered around. It was the same noise as earlier, only a little harder to hear because of the nearby bustle.

Knock, tap, knock.

It sounded as though it was coming from the pavement. To be precise, it was coming from the manhole cover in front of her. Probably a trapped animal, or maybe pipes. That didn't explain why it had been so loud on the first floor of a building fifty metres back down the road. Hannah gave the metal plate a wide berth.

She carried on up the street, only stopping when she reached the Marylebone Road, solid with traffic escaping London at the end of the workday. The tapping sound didn't follow.

Standing on top of the Ouroborus itself, she could feel the linether surging into her. Every time she visited the path of the serpent, the feeling grew stronger. Hannah didn't know what to do with that sensation; it frightened her, but it also connected her to the hidden world that drew her in more and more, every day that passed.

In his final conversation with her, Wayworthy had said there was no word for what she was becoming—someone who controlled the linether, not simply someone who used it like the LineFolk, so what was she?

More than anything else right now, she felt out of control.

Hannah crossed the road and walked to the edge of the park. She sensed the linether fading beneath her feet despite its attempts to follow her. That was good. Getting away from the LineFolk, and remembering what life was like before, was all she wanted at this moment.

She sat on a bench facing the trees and caught her breath, letting her mind go quiet.

"If we learned one thing last year, it was that leaving the Ouroborus does *not* keep you safe."

"Jesus!" Hannah shouted, leaping up as the voice came out of nowhere. "Why the hell are you sneaking up on me, Patel?"

The police officer brushed some lint off his suit jacket cuffs and smiled.

"Where's your leather one gone?" she asked. "I thought they'd welded it onto you."

"Meeting with the boss," he replied. "For obvious reasons, she doesn't want me filing *actual* paper reports and putting them into the system. Plus, I'm only a detective sergeant. That's not a rank that normally gets a one to one with the gaffer, so we have to do it under the radar to avoid questions. Hence, the hour of the day."

"Can't she just promote you?"

"Not without reason, and all the reasons she might have to bump me up to DI are too uncomfortable to make public. So I have to pop in from time to time after hours and fill her in on what you and the rest of the freaks have been up to."

"Don't call them freaks," she insisted.

"I'll stop calling them freaks when they stop doing freaky, stupid things. One of the idiots even grew wings over at Kings Cross a couple of months ago. It's taken me weeks of insisting the footage is AI before the newspapers backed off."

"Whatever. Why are you here? And how did you find me?"

"Your alarm, of course. You didn't think you actually had to press the button for me to see where you are? That's just the Bat-Signal that calls me."

Hannah wasn't sure how she felt about that, but was somewhat reassured to know that Patel, and the resources at his disposal, were always on hand.

"So, what do you want?"

"Matcha, of course."

"If you fancy a drink, all you have to do is text me."

Patel shrugged. "Where's the fun in that? Anyway, I was in the area, so I thought I'd surprise you."

"Consider me surprised."

"Usual place?"

"Not unless you're driving. I'm not walking back to Soho."

"The other usual place, on Baker Street."

They had found a little cafe near the home of the fictional Sherlock Holmes while they were debriefing the events of the night at Golden Square, namely Patel's struggle to explain human body parts strewn beneath the tower. It had become a sanctuary for reflection, mere metres outside of the Ouroborus. They assumed it was blissfully LineFolk-free, and with Hannah's growing ability to sense when one was nearby, they essentially had an early warning system in place.

They strolled west, and Patel turned up his collar as the temperature tipped over from cold to freezing.

"How are the Flynns?" he asked.

"Oh, you know. Axton is doing his best not to turn into Wayworthy 2.0, and Mia is trying to pretend her father didn't catastrophically screw up the Ouroborus and set an ancient Welsh monster onto his own daughter."

"She hasn't seen him since?"

"If she has, she isn't telling me about it."

"No one else has spotted him as far as I know. Not that he put himself in the limelight even in normal times, but now that you've turned him into Mr Ugly, he's not going to be showing up to premieres any time soon. I've heard rumours that his board is getting twitchy about his absence, so I suspect he'll be driven out of hiding sooner rather than later."

"Can't you arrest him?"

"On what grounds? All his building work was legal. He's well-connected and got all the permits. We only managed to get it shut down on technicalities. And how would I charge him with attempted murder? I'd have to reveal that the weapon was a vicious, giant-sized newt."

"Did I do the right thing?" Hannah asked, suddenly stopping on the spot.

Patel catapulted a couple of metres past before he realised that she wasn't with him. He put his hands on his hips. "We'll never know what he would have done next, but it was unlikely that he would have let Flynn destroy the device and all his plans with it unless you had made him stop."

"Yeah, I get that. I suppose I mean, were *we* right to do something so...awful? He thought he was making London safe for the LineFolk, and I nearly killed him."

Patel frowned. "If he was making it safe for anyone, it was for himself. And you know it wouldn't have worked anyway. The result would have been a bloodbath."

"Hurting people doesn't come easily to me."

"Nor should it," Patel said, surprising Hannah by taking her hand and gently pulling her down the road. Then she surprised herself by holding on to it for a few seconds more than necessary. "The history of the LineFolk is violent," he continued, looking dead ahead and not at her. "So the longer that feeling stays alien to you, the better."

He seemed to decide that this topic was too dark and moved on to something else. "Are they at least paying you now?"

"If by 'paying' you mean that Axton lets me go into the petty cash and take whatever I fancy, then, yes."

"Sounds like I might need to tip off the taxman." He punched her shoulder awkwardly, as though he had considered putting his arm around her and then thought twice.

"Sure, if that's the way you want to bring the entire LineFolk secret into the open."

Baker Street was as busy as ever during rush hour. As they passed the Tube station entrance, a gust of warm air flooded out into the chill, and Hannah slowed to enjoy it. Except now she couldn't just feel the warm air; she could feel the linether. It wrapped itself around her, and she felt it stretch like putty, further into the no-go zone than it would normally do. She was like the gravity well of a dying star.

Tap, tap, tap.

"Oh, for God's sake," Hannah exclaimed. "Tell me you can hear that tapping?"

"I just hear the traffic and that busker," he shrugged. "What tapping?"

"I heard it at the clynic, then on the street outside. Now I can hear it here, a mile away."

Tap, tap, tap.

"You seriously didn't catch that? It's like it's right by my head. *In* my head, almost."

Tap, tap, tap.

Hannah put her hands on her temples. "Whatever the hell this is. Stop."

Patel looked concerned. "I think you should go home. Maybe get Flynn to check you over."

"Axton's not a doctor."

"Granted, but what are the chances of you hearing a tapping noise that no one else can, and it's *nothing* to do with the LineFolk? Those are long odds. A regular doctor would give you an MRI, but what you probably need is an exorcism or something like that."

Hannah put her hands on her hips. "You really come out with the most ridiculous nonsense. OK, no matcha tonight. I'll ask Axton. Walk me back?"

Patel didn't say yes, but he bowed slightly and waved her toward the pedestrian crossing across Marylebone Road.

As they walked away from the station, Hannah was sure she heard the tapping again, but this time with a terrible urgency as it faded into the distance.

Chapter 3

When they arrived back at the clynic, Flynn was bustling down the steps to the pavement.

"Hannah, where have you been?" he asked in a frustrated tone, shoving some strange implements into a leather satchel that was hanging around his shoulders.

"Just out," she replied. "It is after hours. You know. Free time."

Flynn looked irritated at the sarcasm. "Yes, I am aware of what hour it is, but I need you urgently."

"Why didn't you call me then? We have a phone in the reception area."

"As you know, I never use a telephone."

Patel pulled a face, and Flynn scowled at him.

"I'm here now," Hannah interjected. "What's wrong? It's not Mia, is it?"

"Mia's completely fine. No, we have a house visit to make. Well, not so much a house visit as a location, but there is a being of concern there who might need us. Specifically, they need you."

"I don't understand. Why me?"

"I'll explain on the way. Come on."

Flynn headed off at a pace that suggested time was of the essence.

Patel looked at Hannah. "I'm not running after him. You're on your own. But remember. Ask him about the knocking in your head."

She tapped her temple with an index finger and scurried to catch up.

"Where are we going?"

"To the southern Edge," he shouted over his shoulder.

"What? On foot? That's a couple of miles."

"I would rather not take the Murderessline. I've never appreciated the dwellers creating such an homage to that woman."

"Who's that?" Hannah drew level. "Why do you always talk in riddles?"

Flynn was confused. "You have spent the last two months with your head in the library, and you don't know about the Murderess?"

"*The* Murderess? No, was she LineFolk?"

Hannah's colleague looked as though he was choking on something. "LineFolk? Of course not! If she were, then she was a traitor to her kind."

"There's a lot of that about. So who was she that's so important, or infamous?"

"Victoria. Your queen. As villainous and fervent a hunter of the LineFolk as ever walked the fields of Albion."

"You really are sounding more and more like Wayworthy every day," Hannah laughed. She imitated him. "A more fervent, wicked, hunting machine, blah, blah."

"This is serious, Hannah," Flynn insisted, weaving around the pedestrians at Oxford Circus, who seemed determined to be wherever he intended to walk. "She devoted vast resources to eradicating the LineFolk from the United Kingdom."

"Queen Victoria knew about the LineFolk?"

"Knew, studied, detested. As did her court. It was a far more...aware time for the dwellers. Luckily, you have all descended back into ignorance."

"She was a dark horse," Hannah said admiringly.

"She was a monster. And I say that having personal knowledge of a lot of beings that you would refer to as monsters. Trust me, she was much worse. An inquisitor, a witch-finder, a eugenicist. Nothing that humans did to each other in that century even comes close to what they did to the LineFolk. It's astonishing that the thaumatagineers, who were responsible for building that line, allowed the dweller authorities to name it after her. Almost like a sick joke."

"OK, so Queen Vic was evil. Does that mean we have to walk all the way to the river just because you don't appreciate the fact that some old men named a Tube line after her?"

"We aren't heading to the river," Flynn informed her. "We are going alarmingly close to the scene of her crimes. Just south of the palace."

"Buckingham Palace?"

"The same."

"Then we are definitely taking the Tube." Hannah hauled Flynn by the arm down into Oxford Circus station. "You have a bank card, don't you?" she asked.

"I have an Oyster thingy," he said, fumbling in his pocket for it and tapping through the barrier. "Although I have no idea how to...fill it up. Mia does that stuff for me."

"Why is Mia the one who gets along better with the dweller world?" Hannah asked, pulling Flynn toward the Victoria Line when it became obvious that he was targeting a convoluted Bakerloo-Circle Line route instead.

"Her father. He is—was—well integrated. She grew up in that environment. Living like a dweller, but also separated from them." He gazed nervously around at the tunnels as they descended the escalator, clearly expecting the spirit of the long-dead queen to come from the walls and drag him to the hell in which he hoped she now lived.

"What about you, Axton? What's your origin story? Tell me about your upbringing."

"I don't have one," he sighed. "Not one worth telling, anyway."

Hannah let it drop. She had spent enough time with the LineFolk to understand that they didn't give up their secrets easily.

Flynn twitched in his seat on the train, and she put a hand on his arm as they travelled. "It will be fine. All old history. Shall we get off at Green Park, or...er...Victoria?"

"Now that you have dragged me down here, it might as well be her station. It's a bit closer to where we are heading."

"Going to fill me in now?"

He looked around the busy carriage. "Not with all these dwellers, no."

The train slid to a stop at Green Park.

Tap, knock, tap.

Hannah swivelled in her seat and peered at the window behind them. It sounded as though someone had been rapping their knuckles against it. There was no one within ten metres. She turned back to look at Flynn and for a signal that he had heard it as well. His face was stony and staring dead ahead.

Tap, tap, tap.

"Oh, come on! You are seriously telling me you can't hear that?"

He glanced around the carriage. "Hear what?"

"The tapping sound. Right behind our heads."

"Sorry, no. These old trains make weird noises."

"We aren't moving yet!"

"You are too jumpy. There wasn't any tapping."

They travelled on in silence to Victoria. Flynn was up and standing at the doors of the train long before it had even begun to decelerate into the station, bolting for the escalators as though the carriage was on fire. As Hannah chased after him, she glanced over her shoulder. The tapping didn't follow.

"Northern exits, please," Flynn insisted. "We are right on the Edge here, and I don't want to take any risks."

"So, now will you tell me what we're doing?" Hannah pleaded.

"Yes, but don't ask questions as we go. The Ouroborus cuts over several roads on the southern Edge, and I need to concentrate as we walk or I'll accidentally stray."

"Stray cat," Hannah chortled, but when she saw Flynn's face, she mimed a zipping motion across her lips. Although Mia occasionally allowed a joke about her feline nature, and in fact sometimes she poked fun at herself, Flynn took his cat-persona far too seriously.

"We are going to see a ghost."

"Fuck off!"

"Hannah! I told you not to interrupt." Flynn slammed on the brakes and folded his arms.

"Sorry, but you said we were going to see a ghost! What am I supposed to do? Just nod sagely?"

"You've seen spectrals before. We get the occasional wisp into the clynic. Along similar lines, at least visually."

"Those were just like fuzzy humans. Most of them are virtually solid. The way you said *ghost* suggested this was different."

Flynn cocked his head. "I suppose you're right. In this case, it is a phantasm and therefore not technically LineFolk. Wisps are generated by the linether. Phantasms use an equivalent energy source, but they are very much echoes of dwellers of the past."

"Proper ghosts then. Of dead people."

"Of dead humans, yes."

Hannah smiled. "Well, nothing's ever boring with you, Axton Flynn."

He took this as permission to continue walking, and they wound through the back streets and lanes of Westminster for several minutes. Hannah resisted asking any more questions. She was confident Flynn would spill the beans about their task when the time was right.

He stopped in a narrow road flanked by red brick mansion blocks and townhouses.

"Dartmouth Street. I can go a little way up here, then you are on your own."

"On my own?" Hannah squealed, breaking her silence. "What do you mean, on my own?"

"You can't possibly expect me to step off the Ouroborus?"

"What I was expecting was for you and me to find a misbehaving ghost, work some abclynican voodoo, and then head home for dinner."

Flynn sank into his collar a little in the face of Hannah's anger. "That's what we are going to do, only with the emphasis on you doing the...er...voodoo."

Realisation dawned. "Oh, so you only brought me here because you need me to step off the linepath? That's right, isn't it?"

Flynn squirmed and looked at the pavement as though he hoped it would swallow him up.

Hannah continued the attack. "I was stupid enough to think that you actually wanted to teach me something."

"I do," he protested, "just remotely."

"How's that going to work? You don't even own a mobile phone!"

"I'll shout," he whispered.

Hannah growled at him. "OK, what are we doing here? Correction. What am I doing here?"

Flynn seemed pleased to be moving on from questions about his motives. "The headless lady in the crimson dress. The ghost of Cockpit Steps."

He paused, waiting for Hannah to show that it had all fallen into place. She said nothing.

"The headless lady. She stalks the steps and the fringes of Birdcage Walk. In a red dress."

"Never heard of her."

"For many ghosts, I would say that's a blessing, but this one is harmless as far as we know. A motorist crashed his car into a lamppost after seeing her fifty years ago, and a couple of soldiers reported her appearance a century before that, but generally she keeps to herself."

"That's good."

"Until now."

"Of course. So what's changed?"

Flynn paused while a couple walked past arm in arm. His idea of looking inconspicuous was to find a nearby lamppost interesting enough to examine in great detail, while Hannah tapped a foot impatiently.

"I'm not actually sure," he answered when confident he wouldn't be overheard. "I received word of more and more frequent appearances.

The more energy she has, the more she will manifest. She is clearly feeling...energetic. This is concerning."

Hannah looked at Flynn quizzically. "Don't take this the wrong way, but why are we here? She's not come to us with an illness. If anything, she's feeling frisky. I doubt she's paying. And don't you have specialists in this stuff? LineFolk ghostbusters?"

"We are the specialists."

"OK, so what exactly am I supposed to do? Look for her? Talk to her? If she's got no head, how does she speak?"

Flynn looked bamboozled. "Oh, I hadn't thought of that. I assumed she was voluntarily silent. No reports of her making any sound at all. What do you normally do in these situations?"

"Normally? I wouldn't normally *be* in this situation."

"Well, you'll have to wing it." Flynn rummaged in his satchel. "Take these."

He handed over a bottle with a spray atomiser, like something you might have seen on an Edwardian dressing table, and a sheet of plastic film.

"What's this?"

"If the lady doesn't fully manifest, but you can sense her presence, these might help you to locate her. The spray is phantasmaphobic, and the film is phantasmachromic."

"Am I supposed to know what that means?"

"Her presence will repel the droplets in the spray. If you mist an area, and she's there, you'll see the spray parting vigorously around her. Conversely, if she passes through the film, it will turn black."

"And once I've located her?"

"Observe, Hannah. Observe, then report back to me. I'll be watching from here."

"Fine," she said with irritation. "Go find the ghost, watch her, and defer back to the all-knowing man."

"That's a very unnecessary tone," Flynn bristled.

"It's about time you started training me," Hannah said over her shoulder as she headed up the street. "Rather than treating me like a lackey."

She felt bad as soon as she said it. Flynn didn't take her for granted, and he had his own demons to fight, metaphorical and literal, so it wasn't surprising that sometimes he neglected the commitment to train her. He didn't reply, and she couldn't bring herself to turn around and see his expression.

Fifty yards down the road, it turned to the right, and Hannah could see a flight of stone steps picking its way carefully down between two buildings.

There was nothing to suggest that this was anything other than an exclusive part of London, and she stopped beneath the white-painted arch that marked the start of Cockpit Steps. It looked more like a doorway than an arch, as though the stairs used to be inside a long-demolished building and were now open to the elements.

She turned around and looked at Flynn, watching her impatiently from fifty yards away.

"Anything?" he shouted.

"No, just a normal alleyway, with a stupid name."

"Go into it!"

"Yessir!" Hannah saluted.

"And try not to rely *only* on your eyes and ears."

"What's that supposed to mean?" Hannah muttered to herself and started down the steps, which curved to the left until she was out of sight of Flynn.

As she descended, one tread at a time, the temperature dropped. It was already dark, so that wasn't a result of the shade, but the buildings on either side hung over the alleyway oppressively. This was an unhappy place. She could feel it.

Despite worrying that someone else might take the steps and spot her, she closed her eyes and called behind her with her mind, feeling the linether stretch out from the Ouroborus to meet her halfway. She could sense Flynn standing a yard from the edge of the LinePath. For a brief moment, she could see the cells in his body, the power of the serpent flowing through them, before she became embarrassed by the intrusion and retreated. Her consciousness and point of view floated along Dartmouth Street, elevating yards into the air before dropping beneath the ground to the network of tunnels and ruins that made up old London.

As she started shaking herself out of this almost meditative state, she felt a tug on her thoughts, like someone was holding onto the back of her coat as she tried to walk.

Hannah was new to this and suddenly became all too aware of her lack of experience and her naivety. She struggled to grasp her consciousness and, for a moment, she felt like a drone buzzing around her body before it snapped back and she breathed again.

"Is someone there?" she asked, despite her eyes telling her there was no one. There was a tickle across the back of her neck, and she swatted at it as though it were a fly.

Just because you can't see it, Hannah, doesn't mean it's not there.

She fumbled for the equipment that Flynn had given her, but couldn't get it into the right hands, so she placed the film on the steps by her feet. She pointed the bottle into the air and squeezed several times on the atomising pump. A fine mist of whatever it was filled the alleyway.

Almost immediately, a shape appeared about five yards away, made visible by the droplets scattering apart, but it was indistinct. She gave another few squeezes of the pump, pointing it directly at the space that was mist-free.

This time the shape created was closer, just a couple of yards away. Hannah yelped and stepped backwards towards the arch, dropping the bottle in shock. It fell onto the stone steps and shattered; the shards tumbling to the flagstones at the bottom, where the alley turned to the right.

She looked down at the film, sitting on the steps where she had been standing a moment ago. Gradually, it turned black.

"Hello?" she said shakily. "Is there someone there?"

The air in the alleyway got even colder, and the liquid she had sprayed drifted back towards her, coating her skin in a damp layer that sucked the remaining warmth from her face.

"If there's someone there, can you show yourself?"

It started as a smudge on her eyeballs, which she tried to blink away to prove to herself it wasn't real. Then she became aware that there was something like gauze forming against the brown of the brickwork.

It's been one hundred years since you visited me.

The voice in her head was heavily accented—almost Brummie and certainly not recognisably from London.

She snapped her eyes open, but there was nothing there apart from the sense that she was recovering from staring at a bright light for too long.

Why can't I rest?

Hannah wasn't sure if she could reply, or even how to.

I just want to rest.

"Well, that's something we have in common," Hannah said out loud. "Although you must have me confused with someone else. I'm only thirty-six years old, so I couldn't have visited you a century ago."

Don't torment me.

The blur on the walls moved deliberately, and Hannah was sure that she saw a hand becoming visible, caressing the bricks. Its wrist was wrapped in crimson velvet, and slowly the rest of the arm coalesced out of nothing, as though the night had tried to keep a secret and gave it up on a whim.

The figure of a woman, clothed in a red gown, was standing on the step, her arm still stretched out to the wall on the inside of the curve.

This well is nearly empty, but somehow I'm sustained. I don't know how.

There was nothing from the neck up, as expected, and the words were just hanging in the air, an inch from Hannah's left ear.

"Are you the headless lady?"

Nothing.

"I'm sorry if that's a...personal question."

You were there when it happened, so why make me speak of it?

"You really have got me mixed up with someone else, but I think you are saying yes. I'm Hannah. I've come to find out why you are appearing more often?"

Because I can. Just as I could over a century ago. I know not why, other than that the energy is palpable. I almost feel as though I am strong enough to leave this spot if I choose.

"There is more energy? Linether?"

I know not what that is.

"But you're sort of LineFolk?"

I know not what that is.

"Is it a problem for you? That you are feeling energetic?"

No.

Hannah chose her words carefully. "Is it a problem for us? For dwellers and LineFolk?"

That is for you to determine.

"You are an unhelpful ghost."

And you are an unhelpful ophidian.

"What did you call me?"

Why are you here? If you are looking for the source of the energy, look for the other pits.

"Pits? I don't know what you mean. Like Cock*pit*? Cockpit Steps?"

The years have taken their toll on you.

"Now you are a *rude* and unhelpful ghost."

Leave me be. I can wait another century.

Hannah realised that she was conducting an interrogation blind to any context, or the reasons why she was doing it.

"I'm going to speak to my colleague on the road. Will you still be here if I come back?"

I will always be here until I am released. But not necessarily to you.

Hannah backed away, leaving the film and the remnants of the bottle on the steps. When she reached the top, she tried to walk calmly to the waiting Flynn, but her cadence increased as she went, and by the time she got to him, she was virtually running.

"Well?" he asked. "Did she manifest?"

"With bells on."

"She was wearing bells?"

"Of course she wasn't wearing bloody bells," Hannah snapped. "But she appeared, although a little reluctantly. She seemed to think that I was someone else, and that put her in a bit of a bad mood with me."

"How could you tell?"

"She spoke."

Flynn looked excited. "Hannah, that's wonderful."

"Yes, but she was rude, so I could have done without it."

"What else did she say?"

"That she's not sure why she can appear more, other than she has extra...power. And she told me the answer was in the pits, whatever that means."

Flynn looked at the sky.

"Of course. Why didn't I think of that?"

"Think of what?"

"The pits. It all points to the pits."

He scurried off, leaving Hannah standing with her hands on her hips as a mist rolled in from nowhere and condensed on the surrounding cars.

Chapter 4

To follow Flynn, or return to the headless lady?

Hannah watched the abclynician disappearing in the direction of Victoria station. She looked back at the alleyway. A figure emerged from it, and for a moment, she thought the phantasm was on the move, but it was just a middle-aged man in an overcoat. If the ghost was still there, he definitely hadn't seen her.

He rummaged in his pockets as he stepped onto the pavement, then smiled contentedly as he produced a set of keys and approached a door in a nearby building. Before he could get the key into the lock, Hannah sidled up behind him.

"Excuse me. Do you live here?"

The man spun around in shock, pressing his back against the wooden door while clutching his briefcase to his chest, a horrified expression on his face.

"Oh, I'm sorry," Hannah apologised. "I didn't mean to surprise you."

"Well, don't creep up on people," he said. "Not in the dark, anyway."

"Indeed," Hannah agreed. "There are many things lurking in the dark." She glanced back at the alleyway. "In fact, that's what I was hoping you could help with. The steps over there—Cockpit Steps."

He peered at the archway, as though he hadn't noticed the very route he had just taken to his own house. "What about them?"

"It's an unusual name. Cockpit. Do you know the history?"

"Of course, everyone around here does, although it's rather obvious."

"Not to me. Something to do with aeroplanes? Or the old plague pits?"

He shook his head and blinked as though this was the stupidest thing he had heard in a long time. "Plague? Aeroplanes? No! Not that sort of cockpit. It was a fighting pit for birds. The story is that it was the closest pit to Buckingham Palace and so it saw some very high-profile visitors in its day. The steps are all that's left of it. It was probably on the site where that house over there stands now." He waved toward a nearby building.

"Right. Cockfighting. So why is the headless lady telling me the answer is in the pit?"

"Headless lady?" the man scoffed. "You aren't one of those ghost hunters, are you? I think I'll be moving on. I thought you might be interested in local history, not that you would be a lunatic." He turned and struggled to get the key into the lock.

"So, you've never seen her?"

"I don't believe in ghosts, young lady." He was finally successful and opened the door, stepping quickly into the hallway.

"Not believing in ghosts isn't the same as saying that you haven't seen one."

He paused. "Look. I'll confess that I don't enjoy taking those steps. I jog up rather than saunter. Some places simply give you the willies, right?"

"Thanks for your help. It's just idle curiosity on my part."

"Yes, well, next time don't go sneaking up on people." He shut the door in Hannah's face before she could even acknowledge the instruction.

She walked back to the steps and descended to Birdcage Walk. As she went, she ran a hand along the bricks in the way she had seen the headless lady, now very much invisible, doing as she manifested. She could feel nothing. No linether. No different power. Just rough, cold brick.

But the man had been right. This place gave her the willies in a fashion that minotaurs, octomen, and werecats had failed to do.

The mist had settled over St James's Park, and she could see trees, lit dramatically by streetlights, drifting in and out of view. She crossed the road to the edge of the green space. What had Wayworthy said about it all those weeks ago on their impromptu trip to the NeverHyde? The LineFolk could access parts of the park by following the route of the Jubilee Line, or Fleetline as they referred to it, but the lake at St James's bisected the linepath and passage was impossible.

She looked back at the steps and imagined the headless lady drifting out into the road, scaring anyone who was strolling by on an evening like this. Hannah realised she had come a long way in a short period, and that meeting a ghost had been merely uncomfortable to her, rather than terrifying.

But now that she thought about it, hanging around the edge of a park in the fog was not the safest thing to be doing, so she strode down the road toward Big Ben, where the glow of Westminster station promised to welcome her back to the lines.

However, the closer she got, the louder it became.

Tap, tap, tap.

***

Back at the clynic, Flynn was sitting in the drawing room with a pile of books in front of him.

"Didn't want to wait for me then?" Hannah teased. "And how did you get home so quickly? I took the Tube, and you left only a couple of minutes ahead of me."

He glanced up from whatever he was reading. "I ran, as befits the urgency of the situation."

"Are you wearing glasses?" Hannah scoffed. "Since when?"

He whipped them off the end of his nose. "I've just noticed that it's been getting harder recently."

"Do LineFolk get short-sighted?"

"Evidently, although I'm not clear why, especially as I transformed only a few months ago. That should have been a bit of an anatomical reset."

"Tell me about the cockfighting pits?"

Flynn looked taken aback that she was moving on so quickly from questions of his declining vision.

"That's what I'm researching. It explains why the lady is energised."

He clearly wasn't going to say any more, because he popped the glasses back onto the end of his nose and began reading once more.

"Can you go to a normal optician? Wait. Don't answer that. Why is the lady back?"

"She gets her power from the pit. The Cockpit. I don't know why I didn't think of it before."

"But it's gone. I met a guy who told me that there are no cockfights there any longer. The entire building was demolished, apart from the steps."

"Agreed, although that place reeks of death. It has lingered long after the games ended there." Flynn wiped his brow. A sheen had appeared on his forehead. "Did you know that cats don't really sweat? Just on our paws and lips. This human tendency to sprout water from every surface is annoying, even though I've endured it my whole life."

"Why are you sweating, Axton? It's not hot in here."

"Nerves, I suppose. I don't like where this is heading." Flynn stood up and shut the door to the room, then lowered his voice. "I have no doubt that cockfighting took place all over the city in the past, but the prominent naming of Cockpit Steps was nothing more than a smokescreen for what really went on there, particularly in the nineteenth century."

"The man I met in the street told me that the rich and powerful used to go there to watch cockfights.

"Not *cock*fights, Hannah. *Folk* fights. Gladiatorial combat for the LineFolk. Yet another way the Murderess demonstrated her cruelty to her court."

"That's horrible," Hannah whispered. "But how could she do that in plain sight?"

"At that time, the power of the monarch of England differed greatly from what we see today, and the boundary between the haves and the have-nots was nowhere near as porous as the present."

"You've just discovered this in a book?"

"No, it's there in my memories, the elder-memories, that is. And not a secret from the LineFolk, although not a story you tell the kittens. Can you imagine it? Werecat taking on haemovore. Nymph battling weevil. And like a cockfight, always to the death."

"But it's old history, right?"

"I am reasonably confident that the current dweller royal family does not indulge in the ritualised abuse of the LineFolk. In fact, in today's modern world, I doubt that any wholesale collision of LineFolk and dweller worlds is taking place like it did in the past. It would never stay a secret. Yet, it remains the case that the lady is able to manifest more often."

"She's powered by the energy created by LineFolk death," Hannah said, joining the dots. "You said it was not linether, but an alternative source."

"Yes, a phantasm gains its power from LineFolk misery. The fact that the lady is charging up, as it were, tells me that somewhere, that misery is real again."

"The LineFolk have it hard right now," Hannah reminded him. "Could she just be reacting to things being tough?"

"No, it has to be acute suffering and death. Like it would have been in the pit at Birdcage Walk. That's concerning."

"And you haven't heard rumours of anything like that?"

Flynn shook his head. "No, although I'll confess that I don't have my ear to the ground, especially since I took over the clynic."

"Want me to ask Patel?"

"I fail to understand why you lean on that dweller so much."

"Because he knows stuff, dweller and *LineFolk*, and do I need to remind you what Wayworthy said before he left us? I'm both. So right now, Patel is a good friend to me. He understands, and he cares."

Flynn shrugged. "Just remember that in the end he's not one of us."

"So, what happens next? You disappear into a book for a week?"

"If that's what it takes. Maybe we should return and ask the lady?"

"She made it clear to me that I'm not welcome back. It was odd, almost as though she was confusing me with someone who had done her wrong in the past."

"Phantasms are not just floaty humans. They are echoes. So although there is an illusion of sentience, they are doomed to remember and repeat. She was probably recalling and regurgitating an old conversation."

"Where would you go looking for the source of her new power?"

"Me?" Flynn looked baffled. "I really don't know."

"I can't believe I haven't asked this before, but is there a LineFolk government? Someone who's in charge?"

"Goodness, no," Flynn said, whipping his glasses off again to better glare at Hannah. "There are conventions, of course. Any culture needs those. But how could we have a government? It couldn't operate effectively within a city such as London. LineFolk society is multi-layered, integrated in a myriad of ways with the dwellers, and frankly far too diverse. Of course, there are some with more status than others, which confers a form of power."

"Like Tarrin."

Flynn grimaced. "Yes, like him."

"And you."

"Oh, I suppose now that you mention it, yes."

"Patel once told me that Wayworthy was pivotal for the Line-Folk. Has that mantle passed to you along with his memories?"

"The Master was special, Hannah. You must have sensed that. He had lived through centuries as an abclynican, a mage, and a wise man. There is nothing of note that happened in the last four hundred years that didn't have his fingerprints on it. Right until his final breath. That breeds respect. I fear that the community does not look at me in the same light." Flynn's face told a story of worry. "Have you noticed our footfall is declining?"

"A little," she admitted. "But you *are* him, in a way. Why would anyone care?"

"I feel like an actor playing the part of Julius Wayworthy. Imagine how that comes across to the LineFolk. No, they are taking their patronage elsewhere."

"Where would they go?"

"To Grubb's, of course. There is nowhere else unless you visit a backstreet grifter, and he's only one step above that, anyway."

Hannah had seen and heard the name several times since she had arrived at the clynic. Flynn himself had asked if she attended Grubb's when he didn't immediately recognise her. Patel had mentioned him before. He was also the author, with Wayworthy, of a book in the clynic's library.

"Is he a rival?"

Flynn laughed. "The Master never considered him as such because he was unconcerned about things like how the community perceived him, but I am not so noble."

"They had history," Hannah observed. "The books they wrote together."

"Oh yes. Such history." Flynn adopted a faraway look as though he were leafing through a mental photo-album. "Weird. I rarely feel inherited emotions, but the mention of Grubb has brought back a wave of feelings. Nostalgia, pride, disillusionment. I'm not sure what to do with it all."

"Keep the good ones, and park the rest."

"Yes, very wise." Flynn returned his glasses to his nose and turned a page of his book.

Hannah realised that he was glad not to be talking and stepped out of the room. It occurred to her that since arriving at the clynic, things had been abnormal, even by LineFolk standards. She had nearly been murdered three times in one week, and had stopped Tarrin from enacting a potentially catastrophic plan, but then life had settled into what passed for a regular cadence of professional and civilian normality. Not everything needed to be a conspiracy, an imminent danger, or a reason for her to throw herself into risky situations. If Flynn wanted her help, he would ask. Whatever the situation at Cockpit Steps was heralding, he was the best person to work it out. The weird knocking sound that followed her was probably just something echoing around the city from a building site. Not everything was pre-apocalyptic.

She retired to her room, looked at the ancient tome by her bedside table that was full of LineFolk anatomical drawings, and picked up a trashy paperback instead. It was time to give in to her human side.

Chapter 5

HANNAH CLEANED DOWN HER desk with the supply of wet wipes she had taken to keeping in a drawer. It was all too common for a patient to leave slime, or mucus, or something that defied description, smeared over the cracked leather surface.

The latest oozing LineFolk had gone, leaving just a single customer sitting in the waiting room, a young woman who pulled a hood low over her eyes and was wearing the most shapeless clothing conceivable. She hadn't spoken a word since arriving, not even to give her name. Hannah hadn't pressed. It was obvious that she was deeply unhappy and in some pain, catching her breath as she settled into a chair and hunched forward. Incredible red hair spilled from her hood and onto her lap.

When Flynn was ready, he popped his head out of the consulting room and clocked the nearly empty waiting area. His face fell. Normally, it would be heaving with patients at this time of day. The lure of Grubb was becoming stronger and stronger. He looked expectantly at Hannah.

"Sorry, I'm not sure of this young person's name," she admitted. "I think she's in distress."

"Oh dear," Flynn said, leaving the safety of the doorway to approach the patient. "Are you able to walk into my consulting space? Nurse, perhaps you could help."

Hannah gently touched the woman's arm. "The abclynician is ready for you. Can you stand?"

She raised her gaze, and the hood fell backwards. Her eyes were enormous and deeply set, and it was clear, despite her tired and distraught appearance, that she was incredibly beautiful. She tilted her head in an otherworldly way as though she was processing what Hannah had asked her, but her eyes rolled in their sockets, suggesting the effort of thinking was too much. She slumped to her left.

Hannah caught her and cradled her upright, while steering her head between her legs. The woman's shoulder blades heaved up and down as she gulped air.

"Axton, look," she called. "Her back."

The hoodie, which had looked clean when she arrived, was now soaked in blood. Crimson stripes ran from bottom left to top right as though she had been repeatedly scored with a knife.

"That is not good," Flynn muttered, stating the obvious. He crouched in front of the woman. "We are going to remove your jumper."

"Shouldn't we move her first?" Hannah asked.

"I'm not convinced that what we see here is the full extent of the challenge facing her. I don't want to make things worse."

As Hannah pulled gently at the woman's arm to raise it, she resisted and cradled it to her body, sucking in a sharp breath through clenched teeth.

"Is it painful?" Hannah asked, but got no reply. "I think we'll have to cut your hoodie." She scuttled into the consulting room and found a pair of scissors, slicing carefully up the sleeve to the shoulder and then across to the zip, where she had to squeeze hard to deform the metal to the point where it snapped. The entire time, the woman's head wobbled gently on her shoulders as though her neck muscles had taken a holiday.

The hoodie slid to her waist. Hannah and Flynn exchanged glances. Her arm was clearly broken, and the wounds on her back were only a fraction of the damage to her torso, where the skin was scored with cuts, gashes, and grazes.

"Axton, shouldn't she be in a proper hospital? I've never seen anyone come in here with injuries this severe."

"There are no hospitals for LineFolk any more. Not since..." His voice trailed off until he refocused on the woman. "We can set the break and stitch the wounds."

"And then what? Send her back out into the street? She's too weak to go anywhere. I don't know how she made it here in the first place. And whatever did this to her is probably still out there."

"I am certain what did this to her," Flynn said in a monotone. "It was a cat."

He spread out his fingers in a crude approximation of a clawed paw and dragged them through the air. "Right size. Right shape. I've seen this before."

Hannah asked nothing else, and for the next hour they worked together to patch up the woman as best they could. Despite her resistance, they moved her into the consulting room using the wheelchair that Wayworthy had kept for his rare jaunts out of the safezones.

As they cleaned themselves up at a sink in the corner, Hannah asked, "Why wouldn't we just move her into the no-go zone?" She nodded at the stark, tiled area. "She would transform into her true form, and you've told me in the past that's usually enough to perform some biological reset. Wouldn't that have fixed her?"

"We don't know what she is. I'm fairly certain she's not a nymph. It's her eyes that are the giveaway. They are like pools."

"You noticed as well? Mind you, I'm not surprised. She's gorgeous."

"Her true form might be exceptionally dangerous. We do not turn any LineFolk away, but it helps to understand what you are dealing with first. My experience is that the ones who won't tell you what they are, then cause the most trouble."

"Why couldn't she have just found her own space to transform? Somewhere private."

"I would have done that myself, but many LineFolk are petrified of the change. We spend our entire lives trying not to. To do differently is almost unimaginable for some."

"I think I could manage it in these circumstances."

"There is another possibility. That she is an anthrothrope."

Hannah kicked herself. Of course. She was used to meeting LineFolk for whom appearing human was a radical disguise, but many took that form day in and day out. They had other abilities.

"I suppose that until she's well enough to answer, we'll be in the dark."

"Can't you sense anything? I don't like to ask, but..."

Hannah blinked. "I don't know what I can and can't do yet."

"Why don't you try?"

"Because I'm scared that I won't be able to do it."

Flynn gave her a kind smile of the sort that he hadn't given for some time. "I think you are plenty brave enough. If it doesn't work, it means nothing. Simply that you need more time to learn."

Hannah gathered herself. "OK, I'll have a go."

The woman was lying on her side on the sofa, her broken arm laid carefully on the cushions. Hannah knelt beside her and placed a hand on her good shoulder. The linether swirled happily around, dancing with delight as she breathed it in and out.

Darkness.

At first she thought it was an absence of anything, but gradually she realised it was simply the absence of light. She felt an embrace of something, wrapping her in a cold but pleasant blanket. She gently drifted back and forth like a cork on the ocean.

"Water," Hannah said.

"Go on," Flynn encouraged.

"There's nothing else to say. I just sense water. And a feeling of enormous loss. Yearning. She *longs* for the water." She concentrated hard. "There's something else. I don't feel the linether in her, not in the way I normally would with disguised LineFolk."

"That does not fit with the anthrothrope theory. To have that desire to be in the water would suggest therianthropic tendencies of an aquatic nature, although I'll confess I don't know what to make of the absence of linether."

"You mean she's a mermaid."

"There are no mermaids in the Ouroborus."

"I notice you qualified that with *in the Ouroborus*, but point taken. So she's probably a therianthrope who couldn't get to a no-go zone to change and do some self-repair."

Flynn dried his hands on a cloth and put them on his hips. "No matter for now. The important thing is that she's out of danger. The immediate problem is what to do with her. I don't want to move her somewhere else in the building. Frankly, I don't want her near the kittens until we know more."

"You aren't thinking of throwing her out, are you?"

"Not at all. But I think that you and I should take turns watching her. I'm happy to stay here for the first shift if you would like to rest."

Hannah was appreciative. Dabbling with her powers had given her a headache that probably needed a dark room and some quiet.

"Give me a couple of hours. I'll bring you some food when I come back."

***

Flynn hadn't moved when Hannah returned. He was staring at the sleeping woman, who had shifted onto her other side and now had her back to the room.

"How's she doing?"

"OK. Still hasn't said a word to me, although she opened her eyes long enough to turn over. I think she's dozing, but to be honest, she might just be listening to us."

Hannah handed him a plate of biscuits. "Here, this is the last of them. You and Mia need to up your snack game. Julius always kept a well-stocked cupboard."

"The children steal them."

"Talking of the children, they're heading to bed. If you go now, you'll catch them."

Flynn gave a final glance at their patient and left. Hannah settled down into the armchair. She had brought a couple of books from the library, including her trusty bestiary that was rapidly becoming her reference for LineFolk species.

"Has he gone?" The sudden words made her drop the books in shock.

The woman gingerly turned herself around and looked at Hannah.

"Oh, you *are* awake. If you mean the abclynician, yes, he's left the room."

"Good." Her accent was Scottish, which caught Hannah by surprise. All the LineFolk Hannah had met so far had London accents—hardly surprising when they had been hiding in the city for years.

"That's a little unfair, seeing as he's the one who just patched you up."

The woman pulled a doubtful face and winced. Flynn placed a lot of faith in the potions that he concocted in a large apothecary's cabinet and seemed to have no time for the over-the-counter painkillers that Hannah would have dispensed to take the edge off a broken limb. The woman's eyes glazed slightly as though she was having trouble focussing, not at all surprising considering her condition.

"Were you quiet earlier because of the pain, or because of the abclynician?"

"Please don't send me away!"

"I'm not going to."

"I heard you talking to him about it."

"Yes," Hannah said patiently, "and you know that we also said that you were in no position to leave. So, here we are." She motioned to show that she wanted to check the dressings, and the woman nodded her consent.

"No one can know that I'm here." She coughed and held her chest with her good hand, leading Hannah to wonder if she had internal injuries that they hadn't spotted.

"I know that this is a world of secrets, but do you mind my asking why?"

"They think I'm dead." She looked desperately into Hannah's eyes.

"Who is *they*?"

The woman shook her head.

"OK, what brought you here?"

"Isn't that obvious? I'm broken." Her voice was light, ethereal, and melodic.

Hannah wrinkled her nose. "You know what I'm asking."

"Grubb threw me out."

Oh great. The only ones who come here now are Grubb's rejects.

"I woke up in the street, his man standing over me. He told me to...crawl away and die."

"And you crawled here instead."

"I had nowhere else to go."

"So you were refused treatment at the other place? They are picking and choosing who they help?"

"I don't know. I don't remember being taken there. Someone must have, though."

She coughed again, and the fit went on for some time. A few specks of blood appeared on the bandage of the hand she used to cover her mouth.

Hannah didn't waste a second calling up the stairs for Flynn. Faced with the abclynician, the woman clammed up once more, and whether through illness or obstinacy, she seemed to go on a downward spiral that saw her lie back onto the sofa and close her eyes.

Hannah and Flynn retired to the waiting room to speak.

"She might have injured a lung," Flynn said. "This is where I'm limited in my diagnostic abilities. The Master would have conjured up a mental X-ray, but I don't have that power."

"Are you sure we can't take her to a human hospital? If she is an anthrothrope, then they'd be able to treat her just fine."

"No way. We will do our best here."

"Grubb wouldn't treat her."

Flynn grabbed Hannah's arm.

"What did you say?"

"She told me that Grubb refused to see her, or at least she thinks he did. She came round lying in the street near his place. Sounds like he's getting picky now that he has siphoned off our patients."

"This is not a case of simple professional misconduct, Hannah. Grubb is as bound by the code never to refuse a patient as I am. That he would do so is very worrying. I had a feeling that she was trouble."

"Hold on, that's quite a leap. She seems nice." Hannah shook herself out of his grip.

"A woman shows up, mute and uncooperative, with some serious wounds that have obviously been caused by an assault of some kind—by a werecat, in fact. She admits that another abclynician refused to treat her. There is nothing normal about this. It would be very helpful if she told us what happened."

"Or we ask Grubb."

"I'm not asking that man anything!"

"OK, I will."

Flynn shook his head. "Sorry, I can't allow that."

Hannah was dumbstruck for a moment. "I'm sorry, what did you say? Are you telling me what I can and cannot do?"

Flynn recoiled a little, as upset by conflict now as he had been when they first met. She could see that he was steeling himself for a fight.

"I am the principal here, and this is your place of work."

"It's gone far beyond being just a place of work, Axton."

He looked contrite. "Yes, it has. But please believe me. Grubb is not our friend."

"Do you have a better suggestion for how we can help her?"

"Yes, we put her up here until she is recovered, then send her on her way."

"Without knowing where she came from? That would be negligent. No, I'm going to Grubb's and asking what he knows. I would telephone, but I imagine that he's as much of a Luddite as the rest of you."

"Fine, but please don't spend a second longer there than you need to."

"You treat him like a rival, but you are both looking after the same community. You should collaborate, not obstruct each other."

"It's not that simple, Hannah. But, as long as I don't have to see him, you can do what you want."

"I'll get my coat."

Chapter 6

IT WAS AN ALMOST imperceptible change, but the atmosphere suggested that spring was around the corner, and walking along the northern edge of Hyde Park in the late evening sun, Hannah's spirits lifted. It felt that ever since she had discovered the LineFolk, London had existed under a blanket of bleak winter gloom, which was entirely appropriate for the urban underbelly she had disturbed. But with a pale blue sky and the temperatures rising, it appeared the hidden city was retreating further into the shadows and no longer threatening to break free.

Flynn hadn't been able to give her an address for Grubb's clynic. He said that it wasn't because he didn't know it, but because it didn't have one. Hannah pointed out that this was impossible, unless Grubb was operating out of the back of a burger van, but Flynn simply rolled his eyes and gave her some instructions to follow when she got to the Edge.

"He's out on the Ouroborus itself. He's never understood why Wayworthy thought he could work effectively with just the Portmanteauline to power him and a no-go zone that was sandwiched between the Portmanteau and the Murderess. His premises are more...basic."

"So how do I find him?"

The notes Flynn had provided were sparse.

Go to the far western extreme of the Corridor.

Look for Linden Gardens, off to the north.

There is an entrance to a private mews at the end of the road.

Ignore the main gate and knock on the small, unmarked door in the wall to the left.

Someone will tell you what to do next.

"And you know this how?"

Flynn tapped the side of his head to imply it was buried somewhere in Wayworthy's memories, but said, "It's not a secret to the LineFolk." Hannah wondered when all these 'secrets known to the LineFolk' would become hers to know as well, now that she was one of the gang.

As she headed out, Flynn had added, "It's not like here."

In Hannah's experience, there was nowhere quite like the clynic, so that wasn't too surprising.

By the time she got close to Notting Hill Gate station, she was regretting the decision to walk. There were times when the Ouroborus felt hopelessly tiny, but today was not one of them; the majestic houses that she passed were clearly well out of the league of all but the most fortunate LineFolk, so this was an area that was safezone in name only, as it was economically off-limits to most. She was glad to be wearing comfortable trainers, even though they were a pair that had seen better days. There were too many moments in the clynic when fluids of uncertain provenance cascaded onto the floor, and so she rarely risked decent shoes at work.

Linden Gardens was a minor road of neat-looking, whitewashed terrace houses. She followed it as it turned left and doubled back on itself. At the apex of the bend she spotted a white archway with a set of black gates, preventing unauthorised access to the exclusive mews behind. Like most similar developments in London, this looked as though it would once have been stables for powerful aristocrats and rich merchants. Now they had become their homes.

What had Flynn said? Ignore the main gate and knock on the door to the left. An imposing brick wall ran down the street from the mews, at least twelve feet high. An alarming construction of rotating blades decorated the top to prevent anyone from scaling it.

"Does Grubb work out of the back gardens?" Hannah whispered to herself.

The door to which Flynn had directed her was tiny—no more than four and a half feet tall. He had said it was small, but not that it was pixie-sized. There was no handle and no knocker. Hannah looked left and right along the street. No one was in sight.

She rapped on the wood twice, feeling unreasonably self-conscious.

It opened immediately, swinging inwards.

"Folk?" asked a voice from within.

"Yes," Hannah ventured, not entirely lying and hoping that being part-LineFolk was included in the category.

"Come in. Been here before? Duck and watch your step. Hold the handle on your left with your right hand and feel for the rungs with your foot."

Hannah peered inside, but the owner of the voice was invisible.

"Hurry up! This is not a 'my door is always open to you' situation."

She fumbled at the frame with her right hand and grasped an iron bar embedded in the brickwork.

"Good, now the feet. It's easier if you come in backwards. It saves any tricky contortions on the ladder itself."

Hannah rotated on the spot, holding tight to the handle and tentatively reached behind with her left foot. It dangled alarmingly in the air and she twitched it around, trying to find the ground.

"Easy. I know I said to hurry, but I don't want to be wiping you off the tracks. What are you? A nymph? You shouldn't be scared of heights."

"Heights?" Hannah exclaimed and looked over her shoulder. She was standing at the edge of a drop. The wall fell away several yards into the gloom of a wide trench between it and the backs of the mews houses. "Woah! Not a garden then."

Her feet found the top rung of the ladder, and she felt below it for the next foothold.

"I'm going down?"

"What do you think?"

She realised the voice was coming from above her head. She looked up to see a compact figure clinging upside down to the wall above the doorway. It was no larger than a child, but had a face that had seen plenty of years.

"Oh, I didn't see you up there."

"Most are more concerned about what's beneath them, as should you be. Watch your step on the way."

"What are you?"

It scratched its nose. "Are you sure you are LineFolk?"

"Newly anointed, but yes, I am official. You can touch me if you like." She held out her free hand, hoping that this creature would feel the same thing as Mia had done the night in the square.

It chose not to check. "I'm a gargouille, of course, guarding the door."

"You're a gargoyle?"

"Not a gar-goyle. A gargouille." It adopted a French accent.

"I'm afraid I'm not sure of the difference."

The creature looked confused. "One is a stone carving at the end of a drainpipe, and the other is me. You know, a defender against evil spirits." It stretched its mouth wide open. "Devourer of demons."

"I didn't know, actually."

"Well, Mrs Clueless, take your ignorance and get down the ladder quickly. Unless you want to put yourself in the way of the train that's just left Bayswater."

"What?" Hannah peered down into the darkness beneath her. There was a metallic glint in the dim light. "Are those tracks?"

"Of course they are tracks. You are right on top of the Ouroborus. Couldn't be much closer, to be honest."

"And I'm supposed to go down there?"

"The Master isn't going to climb the ladder and meet you halfway."

She took another couple of steps down until her waist was at street level.

"Oh," sighed the gargouille. "Too late."

Hannah became aware of a rush of wind from below, and the iron-work hummed. There was a screech of brakes from the darkness to her left.

"I wouldn't descend any further if I were you. I think your toes are probably safe."

"Probably?!" Hannah exclaimed and pressed herself as tightly to the wall as she could. She was torn between climbing up or making herself as shallow as possible, and went with the plan to become one with the bricks.

The ground beneath her suddenly lit up in the headlights of the oncoming train. She risked a glance to her left and saw it emerge from a tunnel under the road, the destination sign glowing bright—**Circle Line via High Street Kensington**. It was only a couple of feet below her, and she raised herself up onto tiptoes as it thundered below. She counted the clack of the bogies on the rails as it went, but lost count soon after ten, and so she held her breath until it had passed. Litter tumbled along behind it, caught in the vacuum of displaced air, and the tracks rattled long after it had gone. She still wasn't breathing as she heard a faint announcement drift up from Notting Hill Gate, a hundred yards away.

"Next one is probably only a minute off," the gargouille muttered. "Now's your chance."

"But the rails are electrified!"

"Better watch where you put your feet then. When you get down there, turn to your left and walk up the tunnel. Run your hand along the wall. When you feel the brick become smooth, like polished stone, walk directly across the tracks, then you are there."

"I'm where?"

"Grubb's of course. There is another door on the other side. Don't knock this time; just push it and walk in. Now go. I can hear a train coming."

As soon as Hannah's head was below street level, the door to the road slammed shut, and the creature scuttled across the vertical wall as easily as if it had been on the flat. It pressed its eye against a peephole that she hadn't spotted from the other side.

She continued downward until she felt solid ground beneath her feet. The tracks were laid on stone ballast, and it was uneven underfoot. The light was dim, little of the evening spring sunshine finding its way through overhanging buildings and the depths of the railway cutting. She turned left and walked carefully into the darkness of the tunnel below the street.

Behind, in the distant station, the sound of beeping echoed off the walls. The clockwise train was departing. The tracks furthest from her rattled as it pulled away, and a moaning sound filled the void as it accelerated towards her.

"It won't hit you. It won't hit you," she chanted, knowing that it would be many metres to the left when it passed, but needing to reassure herself. Would she be spotted by the driver or the passengers? The bricks beneath her hand were rough, and her nails caught as she dragged it along on her right. The darkness of the tunnel, as scary as it was, was nothing compared to how terrifying it became when the train's lights appeared behind her, casting her shadow against a patchwork of ancient walls, signs, cables, and other abandoned detritus, yards under the ground.

With a banshee-like screech, the train was on her. She crouched, face turned to the wall, feeling rubbish flicking against her legs and the back of her head. Why was it so long? She regretted not tying up her hair, and it whipped across her cheeks, dancing in the maelstrom of air being thrown around her. It felt as though it took an eternity to pass, and then the tunnel descended into silence as quickly as that calm had been breached.

Hannah coughed and brushed lint, twigs, and goodness-knows-what from her shoulders. She didn't want to go through that again and hurriedly found the wall to her right once more, shuffling forward until the rough brick became smooth. She turned to look at the opposite side. In the gloom, the only things visible were the tracks catching the dim light from the cutting twenty yards away. Four rails per direction, eight in total—four for the wheels, four for the electricity. But which was which? She decided that avoiding all of them was the best policy, but in the darkness it was nearly impossible to see her feet.

She pulled out her phone and switched on the torch.

"No lights!" screamed the gargouille from the rear. "It shows up on the cameras."

"Screw that," Hannah muttered and walked gingerly across the first rail. From the south, she could hear the brakes of another train pulling into Notting Hill Gate. She had only a minute.

She was sure the high-voltage rails alternated with the safe ones. There was a gap of less than a yard between them, but to step over in one go would mean striding across four at once, well beyond her capability. She would need to tread in between.

Hannah performed an exaggerated stride into the space between the first live and running rails, taking care to bring her trailing leg as high in the air as she could. She stood for a moment, pinned between the two sets.

"It's coming," the gargouille cackled, now finding her caution highly amusing.

"Oh God," Hannah exclaimed and took a tiny step closer to the next electrified rail.

"No time!"

Tap. Tap. Tap.

The wind started to blow across her cheeks.

"Hurry up. Grubb doesn't want to be stitching pieces back onto you."

TapTapTapTapTap.

She closed her eyes and stepped again, taking such a long stride that her rear ankle bent dangerously close to the tracks. She was certain she could feel the nylon in her trousers dancing under the influence of the current. For a moment she paused, one leg safe, and the other very much not. Then she hauled herself forward, skipping over rail after rail until she was standing safely.

In the relief of not being dead, she forgot she was still next to an active railway track. She was sure she heard the gargouille mutter, "Oh, I give up," but it was drowned out by the screech of the approaching train.

"Shit!" Hannah scampered across the ballast and thudded into the tunnel wall, except it wasn't brick, it was wood, and it shifted slightly with her weight.

The door. She pushed hard, and it opened slowly. It was heavy, far thicker than she expected, but open it did, just a few inches at first, and then more as she gathered momentum. The train was nearly upon her, but she squeezed her body into the gap between the door and its frame, falling inside in desperation, followed by newspapers, crisp packets, and plastic bags.

"I suppose you think I'll sweep all that mess up," said a voice. "Did that stupid gargouille let you try to enter while there are trains backed up all around the Ouroborus? It's been one a minute for the last hour."

Hannah picked herself up off the ground.

"And shut the door before the next one comes."

She was in a long corridor, with bare concrete surfaces and a tangle of cables and junction boxes. A suspended fluorescent strip light swung, still moving in the breeze from the train. There was a desk that had seen better days placed parallel to the walls, with a man sitting behind it. He flicked performatively through a notebook in front of him. "But luckily for you, the fact that no one else is dumb enough to come during a tailback means we can fit you in quickly. Name?"

"Oh," Hannah said. "You're me."

"I am most definitely me, so you can't use my name. I'll need yours."

"Hannah."

The receptionist wrote that down and looked at her encouragingly. She felt his pain. The number of patients at the clynic who didn't provide a surname always caught her out.

Then she did something reckless.

"Wayworthy."

He didn't write that down.

"Wayworthy?"

"Yes."

"A relation?"

"Sort of."

"Decided to jump ship now that the old man...has moved on?"

She shook her head. "No, nothing like that. In fact, I work there."

"What is this? Some form of inter-clynic diplomacy? A company outing?" He paused. "Industrial espionage?"

"I have to speak to Grubb."

"The Master is busy."

"That seems unlikely, seeing as you told me you are unusually quiet right now."

"He is busy to anyone from Wayworthy's."

"What is it with you lot? Flynn is the same. Every time I mention Grubb's name, he acts like he's drunk vinegar. Aren't you both on the same side?"

"It's not a question of sides, but I assure you, the Master will not have time for you today."

"Listen, I just narrowly avoided getting hit by a train to get here. I would appreciate a few minutes. That's all. We have a mutual patient."

The receptionist laughed. "Yes, more than normal thanks to Mr Flynn driving everyone away with his incompetence."

There was a cough behind them. A man had appeared from a doorway at the end of the corridor. "Silas, don't be rude about the youthful exuberance of Axton Flynn. Give him a couple of centuries, and I reckon he'll be capable." He frowned exaggeratedly. "Oh, he's a werecat. He doesn't have centuries."

"And who are you?" Hannah snapped, having had just about enough of the snide comments.

"The one you're after. I'm Trevillian Grubb."

"You are Old Grubb? You don't look a day over thirty!" He really didn't, although he had a refined way of speaking that harked back to a bygone era.

"Age and appearance are entirely unconnected in my world, Miss...?"

"Hannah."

"She said she's a Wayworthy," the receptionist chimed in.

"Did she? Does that dirty old dog have a daughter?"

"If he did, it wasn't me!"

"Well, whatever may be the case, why are *you* using his name?"

"Got me noticed, didn't it?"

Grubb took a moment to process this, then nodded in appreciation. "Fair enough, young lady. You'd best come into my office."

Grubb's consulting room was little more than a dusty cupboard, lined with electrical equipment in gun-metal grey boxes that looked as though it had last been switched on in the fifties. The ceiling was strangely high, almost two regular stories in fact. It appeared that the floor of whatever was above had fallen through at some point in the past. He smiled curiously at Hannah as he stood aside to wave her in, enjoying her confusion. Broken tiles hung from the walls, and tattered posters fluttered in the breeze from her passing.

"Not what you were expecting? It's a tad different from number fifty, isn't it?"

"Only Flynn and I refer to the abclynic as number fifty."

"Don't make the mistake of thinking you are the only ones who were ever welcome there."

He nodded at a plastic chair, which looked as though it had escaped from a village hall.

"No need to look so snobbish," he chastised. "Someone had to handle the cases that didn't feel happy relying on Julius, and many of them are only comfortable in surroundings that are more basic."

"I'm fine with basic," Hannah said, "but I'm wondering how you work here. There's no space." She ran a finger across his desk. "No hygiene."

Grubb pointed to his right. "The no-go chamber. Just through there."

It was nothing short of a blast door, at least four inches thick and with large bolts that were engaged with a lever two feet long.

"This whole area connects with air-raid shelters from the Cold War period. This equipment around us probably served some such purpose. The size of that door now reassures me that should a patient get out of control, I can contain them."

"So, we are on the Edge here?"

"Right on it. In fact, just a yard to your left, give or take a few inches." He leaned toward her. "You aren't a therian, are you?"

Hannah shook her head. "No, I'm anthropomorph."

Grubb sat back in his chair. "Ah, that term has sadly fallen out of favour, although I am very fond of it myself."

"I know," Hannah said. "I read your book."

"Books, plural, young lady. I have written several."

"I've only found one. You co-wrote it with Wayworthy." He stretched in his seat and, for the first time, Hannah noticed a tattoo on his neck. It was a snake wrapped all the way around. The two ends met just below his Adam's apple, where the head was biting the tail.

"Ah, yes, Brief Essays And Other Papers Concerning the Other-Folk Of Albion And Their Habits and Curious Physiologies. That was our only collaboration."

"So you must have got along at some point," Hannah suggested. Grubb shrugged in a way that was almost petulant. "And you *really* sound like him," she added.

"Why are you here, Miss Chadwick?" Hannah was suddenly taken back to her first morning at number fifty when Wayworthy had asked her exactly the same question, in just as abrupt a fashion.

"I have a query about a patient. Someone we're caring for, but whom I think you saw originally."

"Go on."

"Young woman, at least, that's how she presented to us. Red hair. Broken arm. Deep wounds. A little out of it."

Grubb looked as though he had swallowed a fly.

"You recognise her," Hannah realised.

"She was most definitely not a patient. I'm afraid that I couldn't allow that risk."

"So, that boast that you accept the patients that we can't keep happy was just bravado? You are selective."

"Only in exceptional circumstances," Grubb insisted. "Sometimes it is best to let nature take its course."

Hannah was shocked. "That makes you sound more like a zookeeper than an abclynican."

"It says only that I have a healthy sense of self-preservation and no desire to annoy those who have the power around here. Julius always pretended that he could make a difference, that somehow fairness would triumph over selfishness. He put himself out there time and time again, and look where it got him. I prefer not to ruffle feathers."

"Whose feathers would you be ruffling by helping an injured woman?"

"Someone who wouldn't want the cause of those injuries becoming common knowledge amongst the LineFolk. She was presented to me as dead, you know that? I was just...disposing of the body. Recycling it, you might say. But, as you saw, she was very much alive. Exceptional reserves of strength to survive. I wanted nothing to do with a living selkie. I don't need to get involved in that slavery, and I certainly wasn't going to be responsible for nursing her back to health so she could tell everyone what had happened."

"Where have I heard that word? Selkie."

"If you've read 'Brief Essays', then you can't have avoided it. It obviously made *such* an impression on you." He looked disappointed.

"Type of LineFolk?"

"Indeed, but rather hard to categorise. Some say not LineFolk at all. Therianthrope in nature, but with a unique method of transforming. As related to a regular therianthrope as a mammal would be to a marsupial."

"Tell me more."

"A selkie lives a life between human and seal forms."

"The ocean. It's why I sensed the ocean. She misses the sea so much."

Grubb looked impressed but continued.

"Selkies mourn for the sea when they are in human form. They mourned for it when they crawled onto the beaches of Alba, knowing they could return whenever they liked, but they mourn for it even more if they are trapped inside the Ouroborus. Nothing quite like it. A minotaur doesn't long for grassy fields, or a werecat for the plains of Africa, but a selkie will never be complete on the land."

"You described it as slavery."

"Yes, the method of transformation exposes them to a particular risk. They shed their sealskins. Sloughs right off like a bear rug, revealing a human beneath. And to return to the sea, they reapply their skin." Grubb adopted a hushed tone. "But what happens if someone takes that pelt? The selkie is trapped in human form. They are in bondage to the thief. Servitude. They will do anything, and I mean anything, to preserve a chance that they might one day be allowed to go back to the sea, as a seal."

He shook his head as if resetting his thoughts. "Anyway, that is all colour that I didn't have to give you. I'm having nothing to do with her, and if you have any sense, neither should you, or the boy, Flynn."

Hannah stood up. "You truly are one of the most patronising men I've ever met, and the most spineless."

"Hah!" Grubb seemed unbothered by her insult. "Did you know that there are many LineFolk who genuinely have no spine, more of a notochord at best? It makes for an interesting transformation into human form. They quite literally grow a backbone."

"Where did she get those injuries, Mr Grubb?"

"If I were keen for her not to talk about that, then why on earth would I tell you? It's time for you to leave." He stood up and laughed. "You'll be pleased to know that we operate a one-way system. The path out is rather more straightforward than the route in."

"You called me Chadwick a moment ago," Hannah said bluntly. "I didn't say my real name. I told you it was Wayworthy."

"Miss Chadwick," Grubb smiled. "Your days of blessed anonymity have been behind you for some time. Be careful who knows where to find you. Without my brother to protect you, I suspect your dalliance with the LineFolk will be brief."

Chapter 7

"BROTHER?!" HANNAH SHOUTED AT Flynn. "Did you know this?"

"Of course I knew," Flynn sighed. "I have his memories."

"Did you know it *before* the mind transplant?"

"Yes."

"And you didn't think it was sensible to tell me when you packed me off to the secret clynic hiding on top of the Circle Line?"

Flynn appeared exasperated. "I told you *not* to go! It was you who insisted. Anyway, would it have stopped you if I *had* dug my heels in?"

"No, but not knowing that in advance made me look a right idiot. How was I supposed to get what I needed when I was gawping at him like a guppy?"

Flynn shut the door to the consulting room, where the red-haired woman was still sleeping on the sofa. "Let's not fight in front of the patient."

Hannah threw her hands up in despair. Grubb had ejected her, slightly stunned by his threat, toward an exit that threaded through abandoned service tunnels alongside the underground line and eventually emerged just to the north of Notting Hill Gate station, between two shops.

"It's been a pleasure," he had said, in a voice that suggested he was mildly intrigued by her, but that her interrogation hadn't been how he wanted to spend his evening.

"How is a man who looks to be in his thirties actually Wayworthy's brother?" Hannah asked Flynn. "And does that technically make him *your* brother?"

"The Master was several hundred years old, yet appeared to be in his seventies. Besides, the word 'brother' is doing a lot of heavy lifting. It's not their physical forms that were related. It's their minds."

"So, he *is* your brother!" Hannah exclaimed.

"Remember that I am the first therianthrope to receive the mantle of abclynician in recorded history. I imagine Mr Grubb believes his brother to be dead."

"He didn't seem upset about it."

Did Flynn flinch a little?

"First, in this world, death is not necessarily a permanent state. You just have to look at the headless lady to see that. Second, the Master and his brother had a significant falling out in recent times. Give it a century or two, and assuming I pass the baton to an anthrothrope when my time comes, I'm sure they'll reconcile. History tells us they—we—will."

"Sometimes I wonder if Wayworthy is as suppressed in your consciousness as you insist."

"Enough now," Flynn said, sounding annoyed. "What *did* you discover?"

"She's a selkie," Hannah replied bluntly, pointing at the closed door. "Grubb refused to treat her because he doesn't want to annoy whoever she's bonded to by her pelt. He also seemed to think her injuries were caused by something we shouldn't dig into."

Flynn scratched his head. "I wasn't expecting her to be a selkie, but it explains the drive for water and her pulchritudinous appearance."

"Her what now?"

"Her beauty. Despite the trauma. Selkies are renowned for it. It's why they find it so easy to seduce humans."

"What does her being one of those tell us?"

"I haven't encountered many. Rumour has it they still live free, hidden in the seas around the northern islands. They don't require the Ouroborus to disguise themselves on land; they just need to shed their skin, and they pass perfectly well as human. Even breeding with them." Flynn's lip curled as though this were a repulsive idea.

"So why is she in this city?" Hannah asked. "If I were her, I would be a hundred miles away from London unless I had to live here."

"Let's ask." Flynn opened the door, knocking the selkie to the ground. She had been listening from the other side.

"Shite!" she grimaced, holding her broken arm to her chest. "What did you do that for?" Her speech was slurred, but as musical as ever. Flynn helped her up from the floor, and she retreated to the chair in a sulk.

"So, if you were eavesdropping, you'll know that there's no point hiding it any more. We have learned what you are; just not how you ended up in this state."

The selkie pursed her lips, and Hannah saw her glance at the open door as though she was considering bolting. She stepped in front of it to discourage any thoughts of escape.

"OK," the selkie muttered. "I'll answer your questions." Her body language, however, suggested otherwise.

"How about we begin with your name?"

"My name is between me and my entwined." The selkie twirled her red hair around a finger while staring at Flynn, as though she was attempting seduction, but a coughing fit interrupted her and she returned to looking at the floor.

"That's not a good start," Hannah pointed out. "It's just a name."

"Names have power," the selkie insisted. "My entwined has my skin...and my name."

"Was it your 'entwined' who left you for dead at Grubb's?"

The selkie's face fell, and her eyes grew wide as though she were about to cry. "I don't know. I wasn't awake."

Hannah knelt in front of her. "We aren't here to accuse you of anything; we're trying to help. I don't want to call you 'selkie' or 'seal woman' or even just 'you', so how about a name?"

"It's Rua," the selkie whispered. "Spelled R-U-A-D-H. Although that's my human name. My real name can't be written down."

"Thank you," the nurse smiled. "This is Axton, and I'm Hannah. You got yourself here, so you know you are at the abclynican's near Harley Street. The one that used to be known as Wayworthy's."

Ruadh nodded.

"You have a broken arm and some spectacular wounds on your back, your side, and your legs."

Ruadh nodded again and gently touched her ribs with her good hand.

"We were confused, with such serious injuries, why you wouldn't have just snuck into a no-go zone and transformed—doing an anatomical reset—but I guess that's because you don't have your skin."

A tear ran down Ruadh's cheek and paused at the end of her chin as though it was waiting for Hannah's next sentence.

"Grubb thought you were dead, and when it turned out you weren't, he was too scared to treat you. Do you know why?"

Ruadh shook her head.

"No idea at all? How did you get these injuries? Were you attacked?"

"Yes." She nodded earnestly. "I gave as good as I got, though." It seemed she was seeking Hannah's approval.

"Fought back, did you?"

"Do you really not know how I was hurt?" Ruadh asked incredulously. "You aren't just teasing me?"

"How would we?" Flynn gasped. "I can tell it was a cat, but why, I have no idea."

"It was the cage," Ruadh sighed.

Hannah and Flynn exchanged a glance.

"Did you say cage?"

"Aye, the cage. I know. What's a nice girl like me doing in a place like that...?"

"Trust me," Hannah said. "That was not what I was thinking. I've got some more basic thoughts, starting with 'what the hell is the cage'?"

Ruadh wasn't sure what to do with that question. Her eyebrows scrunched up so hard that they met in the middle of her forehead. "You really live a privileged life here, away from the Edge. You would probably be a punter if you ever turned up at the cage."

"Why's that?"

"Because those who have, watch, and those who don't, fight."

Ruadh tried to turn her back in disgust, but it hurt too much, and she settled for putting her head in her hands. Hannah was getting the sense that she was even younger than she appeared, and that her feistiness was just bravado.

"Where is the cage?" Flynn asked. "Near Grubb's?"

Ruadh gave him a dumbfounded look. "Of course not. That part of London is far too posh, although I guess the clientele at the cage might be able to afford it. No, it's on the other side of the Ouroborus, near Liverpool Street. RoseAlley, they call it. Sweet by name, horrible by nature."

"They carried your body all the way from one end of London to the other?" Hannah asked. "How? LineFolk can't risk cars."

"There are ways," Flynn said calmly. "Tunnels that follow a linepath, but aren't used by the Underground. If I were moving a corpse across London—hypothetically, of course—I would use the Messengerline tunnels, the old Mail Rail. Mostly abandoned by the dwellers, apart from a smattering of tourists during the day. It would get you only as far as Paddington, of course, but that's just a short cart ride to Grubb's."

They both looked at Ruadh, who shrugged. "I don't know; I was 'dead', remember."

"They treated you like a piece of meat, in life and in death," Flynn said sadly. "The cage is the pit at Cockpit Steps all over again, isn't it?"

"I don't know what that is. The cage is somewhere you can repay a debt or repent for an indiscretion. If you are lucky enough to be watching, and not fighting, then it's just a place for fun and to lose your money."

"Why were you there, Ruadh? Not there to watch, I think."

The selkie closed her eyes. "I'm sorry, I'm not saying any more. It's complicated. My entwined put me there."

"They don't sound like they had your best interests at heart."

Ruadh curled up into a ball on the armchair, and for all her tough-girl facade, Hannah saw a tear run down her cheek and soak into the soft material as though she wished it would wick away her pain.

***

"We have to go and see what this cage is," Flynn insisted as he and Hannah climbed the stairs to the living quarters. He had gently closed the door to the consulting room and left Ruadh to cry in the chair before quietly locking her in. "We can't take any risks," he had said in response to Hannah's surprised look.

"Why go?" she asked. "We can guess what it is. LineFolk fighting LineFolk for sport. She's made that clear."

"Can we be sure? She doesn't seem the most trustworthy witness. She has also been through a traumatic experience, however it happened. Maybe it was her 'entwined' that harmed her, and she is covering for them with this fantastical story. Yes, that's probably it. She is merely a victim of a weird sort of domestic violence. You've heard the way she refers to them. It's almost sensual."

"Merely a victim of domestic violence?" Hannah said, feeling for the moment as though she was as far from understanding the mind of a werecat as she had ever been. "I don't think Mia would like to hear you say that. Ruadh was beaten half to death. Anyway, it all makes sense. What we have downstairs is a picture of LineFolk misery. Multiply that a hundredfold, and I bet it would be enough to make the headless lady bouncy again for the first time in years."

"Aren't you curious to see it?" Flynn asked.

"A cage-fight? Not really, are you?"

"Of course I am."

"When you talked about the pit at Birdcage Walk, you sounded as though you found it repulsive."

"I did. I do, I mean."

"So what's different here?"

Flynn cocked his head. "I forget sometimes that you are a dweller by upbringing. The issue is not the practice of fighting to the death, although I must admit it is a little distasteful. The concern with the pit at Birdcage is that it was *dwellers* who made us do it. We were fighting and dying for *their* entertainment. What the selkie has described so far sounds more like a LineFolk matter."

"That makes it OK?"

"It makes it intriguing."

"Then you are definitely not going to see it," Hannah said, stomping her foot. "I didn't expect to find Axton Flynn lusting for blood. If you want proof, I'll get it for you."

He shook his head. "There are layers upon layers in the world of the LineFolk. You have barely scraped down to level two. This feels like a step too far at the moment. You'll say the wrong thing, or tread on the wrong toes."

"And you won't?" she laughed. "Axton, I saw more in ten years working in the NHS than you've ever seen in this Harley Street oasis."

"She's right," Mia said from the door. "Your place is here with the books, darling. Hannah and I will go to look at this mysterious cage. It'll be like our little trip to the swerves last year."

"And see where that got us," Hannah said with a pinched mouth. "Although we make a great team. I'm the brains and you're the brawn." She gave Mia a faint smile, which the werecat reciprocated.

"How long have you been there, my love?" Flynn asked.

"Long enough to realise that I don't want you heading to a boxing match like one of those drunken trolls you sometimes get in the clynic, all worked up and looking for a fight to burn off the testosterone. Do LineFolk have testosterone?"

"Yes, we have steroid hormones," Flynn said wearily. "Why, when the situation is a little dicey, do you always have to be the one to take the lead?"

"Because, Ax, you will always have twice the intelligence, wisdom, and compassion that I do, but I will always have twice the brawn." She took Hannah's hand and led her to the door, then paused and turned back to Flynn. "Oh, and we will never have a problem with domestic violence in this relationship because you would never dare."

Chapter 8

"THERE ARE POLICE EVERYWHERE," Mia whispered as they crossed the road from Liverpool Street station and slipped into Rose Alley. It was a tight, claustrophobic corridor, only a yard wide, carving through the buildings on either side. Sandwiched between a convenience store and a fried chicken shop, the entrance was no larger than a doorway, and looked for all the world as though it was leading into a nineteenth-century slum. Passersby would never have known it was there.

"There's a police station near here," Hannah replied. "How are they getting away with this right under their noses?"

"Should we have brought Patel?"

"They would never let us in with a cop in tow."

The boundary of the linepath was very close now. Hannah could feel the linether pulling her back towards the safety of the Ouroborus, but she resisted it. Normally the sensation was as if the serpent's power wanted to join her. This time, it was more as though it wanted to get away from whatever awaited them on the Edge.

There was a queue at the end of the alley. If anyone ahead of them had wanted to turn around and leave, it would have required some awkward contortions. As they approached the back of the line, the man at the rear turned and watched them. He seemed jumpy. Hannah nodded.

"You're going to be out of luck. They're full. I'm just hoping some Folk leave before the last fight. I want to win big tonight."

"Right," Hannah said noncommittally. She looked at the end of the alley, where it widened slightly into a forest of air conditioning units and ventilation ducts, like a dirty metal cathedral. The queue was ten long, a mix of men and women, typically atypical like all gatherings of LineFolk.

"Do I know you?" the man asked suspiciously, leaning in toward Hannah, who leaned away just as quickly. He stank of beer, but mainly reeked of desperation.

"Doubt it," she replied and turned her back on him, giving Mia a wide-eyed look.

"First time?" he asked. "You look like this is new to you."

"No," Mia said, "and we don't like questions." In Mia's trademark refined diction, she probably sounded tougher in her head than it came out.

"Ooh," the man cooed. "Sounds to me like you've come to the tradesperson's entrance by mistake. Lovely ladies like you should be at the VIP door."

"Where's that?" Hannah asked.

He tapped his nose. "If you don't know, you aren't one." The queue shuffled forward a little, and he rubbed his hands together with glee. "Getting closer. Good job they keep going until the last one is standing."

He stood thoughtfully for a minute.

"Who've you got your eye on tonight? I heard they shipped a score of Púca over from Ériu. Just stuck them in a horsebox and drove them all the way here. None of the idiot dwellers knew a thing."

"A horse doesn't sound like it's an ideal form for...this." Mia waved at the end of the alleyway.

"You've never come across a Púca then, have you? Horse is just one of their disguises. They can do cat, raven, dog, goat, and...er...rabbit. Not that a bunny would be much use. I can't wait to see a Púca fight. Whoever comes up against that won't know if they are coming or going. One minute it's flying, the next minute it's chewing your ankles." He grinned at Hannah and Mia until deciding that they didn't share his excitement, and he went quiet. "It will be better than last night, though. Whose dumb idea was it to throw a selkie into the cage? She couldn't even turn into a seal without her skin, although it wouldn't have helped her. Who ever heard of a scary seal? That cat ripped her apart, not that it did him any good. Lost the next bout and went home in a crate."

The line shuffled forward another couple of feet.

"I'm starting to get hopeful," the man grinned. "I should have been here sooner, but I couldn't get the cash in time. You have brought dweller cash, right? No bartering wagers allowed."

"We've got cash," Hannah said, then regretted it as the man's eyes flicked to her bag, then at Mia's. Mia preened an eyebrow in a way that was werecat-typical, and the man stepped back half a pace.

"What do you think?" Mia asked Hannah. "Shall we stay in the queue or see if there's another way in? Maybe the VIP entrance?"

"Let's stay. It's moving."

After ten minutes, the queue had shortened to just them and the man in front. A large bouncer type faced them, never taking his eyes off the alleyway. Their companion twitched on the spot, clearly now expecting to get in and not wanting to waste a minute. "How many fights left?" he asked, but got no reply.

Hannah wasn't clear what the signal was that his time had come, but the bouncer suddenly turned to him and said, "Mark?"

It wasn't his name. The man rolled up a sleeve and showed a livid red tattoo that was at most a week old. It was weeping, and the design was hard to make out in the dim light.

Mia turned her back on the bouncer. "Shit, darling," she whispered. "There must be some pre-vetting."

"Hope to see you inside, ladies," the man said cheerily as he rolled down his sleeve. "Remember, if you see a Púca, it's probably worth a punt."

"What do we do?" Mia asked through sealed lips. "We should head back."

"No, not until we've at least tried," Hannah insisted. "If all else fails, we ask *how* we get the mark."

Footsteps behind them heralded new arrivals, a giggling group of girls who had obviously been drinking long before they arrived.

"Oh shit, a queue," one of them slurred. "There's a queue, Mags. A fucking queue."

"We're late, you idiot," another replied, taking a huge swig from a bottle of wine. "Of course there's a queue."

"I think we should just push past," the first girl suggested.

"I don't think so," Mia said firmly. "We've been waiting for an hour."

"Ooh, listen to her," screamed a girl from the back of the gaggle. "She sounds as if she grew up in a palace."

Hannah could sense Mia bristling, even with no fur to bristle.

"Marks," called the bouncer, and just like that, the game was on. Mia swung into action.

"Hello," she beamed. "I can't believe it's our turn at last. Room for me and my friend? Excellent." She went as if to walk past, but he thrust out a large arm and stopped her. Hannah could see Mia sniffing the air in front of her.

"Minotaur? I always say that you bulls are stereotyped into security roles like this. You could do so much more."

"Mark," the minotaur insisted, wrinkling his nose and snorting into the damp night air.

"If we were to need to get a mark, where, hypothetically, would we get one?"

The minotaur could tell where this was going, and gestured one of the girls forward. "Mark? You can't all get in at once, though. I have two slots going, so decide who's missing out."

The wine-swigger pushed past Mia with a leery grin on her face and stumbled against the bouncer. She tried to put the bottle down carefully, but misjudged and smashed it hard against the flagstone, where it shattered, showering her, Mia, and the bouncer in red wine.

"Fuck, you idiot," he roared, reaching down to wipe wine off his shoes. At which point the girl vomited. It cascaded onto the back of his neck, pink and frothy. All the while she desperately tried to roll up her sleeve to show off her tattoo.

He roared again and shoved her backwards, wiping ineffectively at his collar.

"I've got the mark," she screamed, thrusting her arm at him.

"Me too," said another girl, and suddenly there was a scrum of drunk women, pushing at the disgusted minotaur.

"Just fuck off, will you?" he growled. "Go in, all of you."

Mia gave Hannah an incredulous look, but wasted no time and pulled her past the angry bouncer and into the darkness of the doorway behind him.

The smell was horrendous, but it wasn't just bad; it was also a charged mix of fear and lust. Ahead, the rumble from a crowd rose and fell in waves, swelling and subsiding in rhythm with the bark of an announcer. Mia squeezed Hannah's hand tightly.

They entered the chamber through a slatted plastic curtain, its translucent strips partially obscuring the commotion beyond. It felt like smacking into a wall of noise and chaos. They stood at the back of a decaying theatre. Rows of threadbare velvet seating stretched down to a stage. In front of them was an audience of hundreds of LineFolk, talking, shouting, eating, and mostly not watching what was happening within the proscenium.

The lighting was poor, although bright spotlights were trained onto the stage, where a square cage filled the arch. A crew of nymphs, wings fully extended, was sweeping sawdust across the floor. They hovered just centimetres from the ground, but generated a noise like a fleet of lawnmowers.

"Look," Mia exclaimed. "Their wings. The stage must be off the side of the Edge."

"And they aren't afraid to be there," Hannah said, eyes roaming over the crowd, all of whom appeared eclectically human. Bookmakers strolled up and down the aisles, blackboards slung around their necks, showing the odds for the next bout. They called as they went, encouraging the audience to part with their cash.

"Where shall we sit?" Mia asked.

The auditorium was not full, but a constant stream came and went, giving it the appearance of a heaving anthill and making it hard to pick out a free spot.

"We don't need to sit at all," Hannah suggested. "Just watch what happens."

"I feel exposed standing here—like everyone is looking at us."

"No one is looking at us."

The announcer's patter built to a frenzy of excitement.

"Wowie, ladies and gentlefolk, that was a ripper of a match, and I mean ripper. Did you see what he did to those wings? Who knew they would keep fluttering after they were...removed from their owner?"

The crowd roared with laughter. It was ugly, and Hannah felt the lustful cruelty reverberate through her bones.

"You only have a minute or two to place your next bet. Don't leave with spare cash in your pockets tonight. Go big and *then* go home. And the next bout is biiiiiiig!"

The crowd roared again, and this time the bloodlust was deeper than the amusement.

"You've told us that you want to see more...mass. Fewer claws. More crushing. Well, you *pressured* us into it."

The audience groaned.

"Look up," Mia said, and pointed at one of the theatre boxes. The announcer was there, leaning over the side, with an old-style microphone in his hand. He swept his gaze across the crowd and the stage, pointing at folk that he recognised and mouthing greetings and encouragement.

"Come on!" he pleaded. "The *weight* is nearly over." Cups and assorted rubbish were tossed at the box in delight.

"OK, OK, shush..." He brought a finger to his lips. Surprisingly, the crowd noise settled. "Shush. Let's have some respect for the soon-to-be-departed."

"Do you think he's here every night?" Hannah asked. "Maybe we should try to speak to him about Ruadh?"

The crowd was now so quiet that Hannah's voice was louder than she needed, and Mia jumped and looked around in panic. No one seemed to care. All eyes were now on the stage.

"From Normandy," the announcer called in a deep voice. "Delivered to us only yesterday in a shipping container—yes, we needed something *that* large to get him here. He's aiming to prove that not all ogres are big and stupid. Well, maybe just to prove that they're not stupid. Entering from stage left, Pascaaaaaaaaal."

The crowd roared again and stood in an excited wave. Hannah and Mia darted back and forth, trying to get a line of sight to the stage.

"Four to one on!" screamed a bookmaker in Hannah's ears. "You won't get better than that, and the odds will only get worse for you when everyone sees him for real."

The figure that entered the auditorium was not what Hannah expected. It was a small, rather unimpressive man who looked around nervously as he crossed towards the stage. He was escorted by two large guards, who stopped when they reached the front row of seats and pushed him forward. He tried to dig in his heels and wobbled on the spot.

"What did I tell you, everyone? From foreign parts. He's not used to the Ouroborus. Seems like in just twenty-four hours, he's got a taste for being human. Makes a change from having a taste *for* humans!"

"He doesn't look like he wants to be here," Mia whispered.

"Of course he doesn't," Hannah replied. "Who would do this by choice?"

The crowd started booing as the man tried to back away from the stage, but the guards behind restrained him, lifting him under the arms and throwing him forward. He fell against the mesh of the cage and clung to it, breathing heavily with his eyes closed.

"Oh, oh!" the announcer crowed. "I think Pascal is about to experience his first change back! Let's all be silent and respectful during this important stage of his life. After all, it might not last much longer."

Someone in the auditorium tittered, and there was a chorus of shushing noises. A punter towards the back screamed drunkenly, and a light booing rippled around the room, but it fell silent apart from the patter of the bookies' shoes as they scampered up and down the stairs.

On the stage, the man scratched furiously at his sides, reaching his arms as far around to his back as he could. Then he gagged and put a hand over his mouth, with the other hand on his stomach. There was a popping noise, and his body jerked in time with each sound.

"Looks like his ribs are going, Folks. We all know what that feels like, don't we, therians?"

Pascal thrust his head back, his hands suddenly clawing around the mesh of the cage, and then the back of his T-shirt ripped with a tearing noise that echoed around the quiet auditorium. His body expanded with staccato movements that gained an appreciative ooh from the crowd with every step. The skin across his bare torso became darker, almost grey. At times it was translucent as it stretched, showing pulsing organs beneath, before it caught up with the expansion of the rest of the body and obscured his insides once more.

"What do we think, folks?" the announcer asked. "How big will he get? Have you ever seen an ogre on these shores before? I haven't!"

He was now as large as a compact car, and still growing. His clothing had long since fallen apart, and he was naked. Whatever was going on in his mind, he still felt some modesty, and he curled into a foetal position as best he could to hide himself.

"Has he stopped?" the announcer screamed. "Is that all we get? I've seen bigger trolls!"

The crowd screamed with him, and a shower of beer splattered across the front of the stage and the ogre's back.

"In fact, shall we put that to the test?"

"Yes!" shouted the crowd.

"I said, shall we put that to the test?"

"Yes!" This time it was thunderous.

"Entering from stage right. She's a pocket rocket. As wide as she is tall. Lock up your goats, ladies and gentlefolk, because here comes...Truuuuuundle."

Chapter 9

THE WOMEN EXCHANGED SHOCKED glances.

"Coincidence," Mia said firmly, shaking her head.

Hannah remained quiet. She kept her eyes locked on the side of the stage where a door had opened and through which a guard was trying to haul a struggling shape. The crowd bayed, but the howling transitioned gradually to mocking laughter.

"Don't be shy," the announcer called, leaning over the balcony as far as he could manage without falling.

Slowly, the figure was dragged into the auditorium. It was hard to see clearly what it was, but one thing was certain. It was wearing a changing robe.

"Oh, no," Mia gasped and gripped Hannah's hand.

The last time Hannah had seen Trundle, she had feared that the troll had drowned in the Thames. Now, two months later, she was in a gambling den, seemingly about to fight for her life.

"I don't understand," Hannah whispered. "How is she here? *Why* is she here?"

"Trundle's a magnet for trouble. Getting mixed up with my father was the tip of the iceberg, it seems. It's that naivety of hers."

"What do we do?" the nurse asked, doubting immediately that there was anything that could be done.

Mia looked around the auditorium where the crowd was roaring at the stage, at each other, and to get the attention of the bookmakers who were coming up with some very long odds for Trundle to win whatever was about to ensue.

"There's nothing we can do. This lot would tear us apart, or put us up there next."

At the front of the arena, the guard yanked back the hood of the changing robe, and it was clearly the troll. She wailed to no one in particular. If Pascal had seemed ill-prepared but resigned to be here, Trundle looked terrified and as if she wanted to be anywhere else.

"She's not violent," Hannah said. "How's she going to fight that thing?" The ogre had stopped growing once he reached the size of a campervan, but was now crawling around the front of the stage on all fours as bestial instincts took over. Guards poked him with sharpened scaffolding poles, and he reluctantly backed into the cage itself, finally comfortable with his nudity.

"They are all so coy tonight," the announcer purred. "If they didn't want to come to the cage, they shouldn't have been naughty folk."

"What does he mean by that?" Mia asked. "How does someone end up here?"

A bookmaker passed them, holding out a handful of betting slips. "Who do you fancy, ladies?" he enquired. "The ogre is big, but the troll might have spirit. I'll give you ten to one on her. What do you say?"

"Piss off," Mia muttered, biting her manicured nails. Hannah had never seen her like this in human form. She was usually so controlled.

"What are you here for if you don't want a little wager?" the bookie asked, waving them away dismissively and moving on down the line.

"Hey," Mia called after him. "Who's in charge here?"

He looked back at them suspiciously, then seemed to decide there was no harm in answering. "The Adjudicator," he replied, pointing up at the announcer, who was attempting to lead the crowd in an impromptu song.

"Why are we waiting!" he chorused. "We are suffocating!"

Trundle was dragged backwards by her hood, towards the stage and pulled up the steps. One guard carelessly backed himself into the no-go zone, and Hannah saw him panic as his limbs started to lengthen and fur sprouted from the sides of his face. He threw himself back into the auditorium as though he expected to be forced to fight if he stayed up there any longer. He squatted on the floor and breathed heavily as his transformation abruptly stalled and his animal features reluctantly retreated.

Trundle tried to follow, but she was prodded by a pole, and she fell onto her backside. She stared, terrified, at the ogre, who was just about holding himself together, crouching in the corner of the cage and tightly grasping the mesh of the walls.

"She's going," Mia whispered, and Trundle started to swell. This wasn't the first time Hannah had watched her morph into troll form, although she hadn't ever seen it clearly. Most LineFolk changes were bone-chilling. This bordered on comical, as Trundle inflated in all directions, her skin turning green, and the changing robe billowing out to accommodate her larger size. She gained a foot in height, but that merely brought her to average. Compared to the ogre, she was childlike. Trundle kicked off her shoes before her feet became stuck in them, and they flew into the crowd, who threw them back at her in hysterics. One struck her in the face, and if there had been residual defiance before, it instantly evaporated.

"Good for you that you didn't take it at ten to one," the bookie shouted at them. "Now I've seen her, I'll give you twenty. How's that for a deal?" All around him, the crowd surged forward.

I'll take twenty. She's pathetic—should be thirty.

"It's going to be a bloodbath," Hannah said. "We must get her out of there."

"In you go, little trollie," sang the announcer. "Quick, quick. We've got five more bouts tonight."

"We have to get to him," Mia said. "If anyone can stop this, it's the guy with the mic." She looked around desperately for a way up. There was a door at the rear of the auditorium with an old exit sign dangling precariously above it. "Through there."

They slipped out into a gently sloping corridor. There was no one in sight, and for a moment the walls muffled the chaos in the theatre. The crowd started a countdown—the fight was about to get underway.

"Quick!" Mia trotted down the passageway, trying to recall the layout of the auditorium and the relative position of the boxes. They reached a set of three doors. "He was in the closest one to the stage, right?"

She put a hand on the farthest door. It was locked. She rested an ear on the wood. "He's behind this."

"What do we do?" Hannah asked.

Mia simply knocked.

The muffled sound of counting reached one and then erupted into a furious roar. The bout had begun. Mia knocked again, harder.

The indistinct caterwauling of the announcer paused momentarily. The handle turned, and he opened it with a single hand, eyes still fixed on the stage. He flicked off the microphone. "Bad timing, Maurice. The fight just started, and I don't think it will last long." He toggled the mic back on. "Look at the troll run! What a turn of speed! She can't keep it up forever, though." The mic went off again as Mia put a foot in the door.

"Tell the cop to fuck off," the announcer growled. "Or I'll let everyone know what he is." He half-turned his head. "Oh, shit!"

He tried to push the door shut, but Mia's shoe did its job and it bounced open. The auditorium was raucous, but without his screaming monologue, oddly bearable.

"No punters in the box," he insisted. "If you want to complain about one of the turf accountants, go take it up with them. I'm just the talent." He returned his attention to the bout long enough to scream, "First blood to our froggie friend! Or is he more of a reptile? Come to think of it, what *is* an ogre?"

From below, the bookies were still shouting for business. Trundle's odds were lengthening by the second.

"We're not complaining about a bookie," Mia said. "We want you to stop the fight."

"Ooh, a vicious right hook from Pascal. I guess it's lights out for tiny Trundle." He covered the microphone with his hand. "Only one thing stops a fight in the cage, and that's when a combatant leaves in a box. What's it to you, anyway?"

"She's our friend."

"I'm sorry to hear that. If you had been better friends, perhaps she wouldn't be here in the first place." The crowd gasped, and the announcer turned to the stage. "Look, you made me miss that. But it seems like your *friend* Trundle is nearly done."

Hannah ran to the edge of the balcony and leaned over. Trundle was on her back in the centre of the ring, her changing robe in tatters. There was a smear of grey blood where the ogre had dragged her from the mesh of the cage into the middle, and now he stalked her, deciding what to do next.

"You sick fucks," Mia said and tried to snatch the microphone from the announcer's hand. She ended up in a childish wrestling match which, despite the strength she maintained even in human form, was doomed from the start.

He looked at Mia's arms as they struggled. "Hey, where's your mark?" For a moment he stopped fighting as he processed this breakdown in venue security, then screamed, "Maurice!" at the top of his lungs. When he realised that no one would hear over the noise of the crowd, he brought the mic to his lips and shouted again. "Maurice! Come to the box."

The auditorium fell silent, despite the ogre picking Trundle up by the head and yanking her to her feet. The sudden quiet made him stop and blink into the lights.

"Intruders! They don't have the pass." The announcer bolted for the door, but Mia took hold of his jacket and held him back.

"Do you know what I am?" she purred. "I'm a therianthrope."

"You and half the room," the announcer scoffed. "Lady, up here you might as well be a weevil for all I care. In this spot, you're human." He shook out of her grip.

Down in the auditorium, no one knew what to do. Without the remorseless pressure from the box, the charged atmosphere softened, and even the ogre panted, catching his breath with Trundle still suspended from his meaty palm. She wriggled slowly, no longer fully conscious.

"You don't need to do this, Pascal," Hannah shouted to a chorus of boos.

"Finish it, ogre," the announcer whispered into the mic, but amplified, it echoed across the silent chamber.

Hannah closed her eyes. Here in the box, the linether played around her. It darted between her feet and wrapped itself about her arms like a shawl.

On stage, the ogre's lip wobbled. He looked at Trundle, dangling limp from his fingers, and squeezed.

Hannah cast the linether toward the stage like an angler releasing a line. It curved from the box and shimmered around Pascal and Trundle. She could see it as clearly as day, even with her eyes shut.

Every cell in the ogre's body lit up for her. Muscle, fat, nerves. Hannah played it akin to a piano with a million keys and began to reverse his change. She didn't know what degree of control she had. When this had happened in Golden Square on the stormy night in November, it had been pure instinct, and the results were haphazard. This was deliberate, and she had no desire to harm Pascal. Hannah started by imagining the arm. The muscles retreated, and bones popped. Tendons and ligaments couldn't keep up and flopped loosely about their insertions. The ogre couldn't maintain a grip and dropped Trundle to the floor. He grabbed his now tiny limb with a bellow and looked around the auditorium in panic.

With the immediate danger to Trundle gone, Hannah slowed and tried to picture the whole. The linether responded to her, enveloping Pascal in an embrace and letting her tease his shape back to human.

The crowd howled. Before their eyes, and definitely in a no-go zone that should have maintained a bestial form, the ogre's human disguise was reappearing.

The announcer could see what was happening but had no idea that it was Hannah's doing. As the audience screamed and bottles flew, several edged away from the stage, scared of what was causing the ogre's transformation.

"Nothing to worry about, folks," the announcer insisted, but his voice cracked. He slowly lowered the mic. "Are you seeing that?"

Mia *was* seeing it and seized her chance.

She bolted through the door and back to the auditorium, pushing past the LineFolk who were now rushing for the exits in increasing numbers, as though scared that what was happening on stage would somehow infect them.

Trundle was sitting on the floor, nose bleeding and still in troll form. Mia stopped at the edge, aware that the Ouroborus ended just feet away.

"Trundle," she hissed. "It's me, Mia. Can you hear me?"

The troll looked at her. "Mia? Why are you here?"

"Come now. Hannah might not hold it forever."

Trundle looked woozily over to Pascal, who sprawled by the footlights, virtually fully human apart from a lingering tinge to his skin.

"He was going to kill me."

"Yes, he was, so come now and we can get out of here."

The announcer spotted Mia and immediately called for help. "Get that woman away from the stage. This is her doing." Then he glanced at Hannah, standing eyes closed, back to Mia, and then to Hannah again, realisation dawning. "I don't know what you are, but you are going to stop this instant." His words reverberated around the auditorium, and the guards looked left and right, unsure of who was being addressed.

"Trundle, now," Mia insisted, stretching out an arm and sensing the protective embrace of the linether weaken. Her hand twitched as the fingers prepared to change and become more paw-like. She snatched it back.

Trundle pried herself off the ground. She wasn't built for speed in this form, and she wobbled forward. "I am feeling unwell."

"Trundle, so help me serpent, if you don't come now, I will never forgive you."

Back in the box, Hannah stepped away from the lip and glared at the announcer. "Do you run this, or are you only the mouthpiece?"

"Why are you asking *me* the questions?" he spat. "You've just done some freaky-arse shit in my place, and I need to know how you did it."

"So, it is yours," Hannah shrugged. "Thought so. I think you can help me."

"Are you a mage? Or something unheard of? I can see it now. *The Amazing Mindgirl! Fights using her steely gaze.*" He rubbed his hands together with glee.

Hannah ignored him. "Yesterday, you put a selkie in the cage. Ruadh is her name."

He pulled a blank face. "A lot of LineFolk came through yesterday. It was a bumper bill."

"I bet you didn't get many selkies? Just one, I expect."

"Well, yes. Selkies are useless in the cage, even if they have their skin, and why the hell would they be in London if they did."

"So why stick her in there?"

"She died, you know," he said matter-of-factly. "Put up a bit of a fight against the werecat, but it was a mismatch. I don't think the cat's heart was really in it. It wasn't my idea to sanction the match, if I'm honest. I thought it was just a bluff to keep a bond over them, but he insisted. Stupid, if you ask me. Now he's lost the leverage."

"He?"

"Let's talk about how much you could make here? If you can do the..." He waved his hand at the stage. "...do the reversing thingy on demand, then no one could touch you. I would promise to put only the weakest human bodies in, but with the most dangerous LineFolk forms. All you need to do is pop them back into Homo sapiens disguise again, and then give them a good whack while they are wondering what the hell happened. You could rack up ten wins before you notice it, and then I'll pay you off. We don't normally compensate, you understand? It's more of a coercion thing."

Hannah stared at him, speechless. "If you aren't the top dog, who is? Who made you put a selkie in the cage?"

The announcer wagged a finger at her. "If you don't know, I'm not telling. Unless you want to consider getting a mark and joining us." His eyes flicked over her shoulder.

Hannah turned slowly. He had glanced at the box opposite. It was masked with a mesh drape, a dirty net curtain that was stained with cigarette smoke. There was a figure inside that she felt was watching them, but it was too indistinct to see. When it saw her looking straight towards the box, it spun and opened the door behind it.

For a moment it was silhouetted against the light from the corridor outside. A weird chimera of cat and man, mis-proportioned, twisted. Then the door shut, and it was gone.

Hannah froze, open-mouthed, in shock.

Tarrin.

Chapter 10

In the auditorium, Mia had coaxed Trundle off the stage, and the troll was slowly reverting to her human, but still rotund, form. The change was performing the anatomical reset that it often did with the LineFolk, and the damage caused by the ogre was evaporating.

"Mia. I did not expect you to be here."

"I didn't expect to see you here either," Mia replied. "I don't know which is more unlikely."

"They won't let us leave."

"They will," Mia said determinedly, with no clear idea of how she would make that happen.

She glanced up at Hannah, who was staring, unblinking, at the opposite box. "Hannah, let's go!"

Mia's shout snapped Hannah out of her trance. "Is that who runs this place?" she asked aggressively. "Tarrin?"

The announcer smirked, which gave her the answer.

"Why does he have a selkie in bondage? What did he hope to achieve by making her a gladiator?"

Below, the crowd, who had amassed at the back of the auditorium in fear of what was happening, became emboldened now they could see

Trundle being led away. They started calling for the bookies to return their money, then erupted in rage when they realised the bookies had all vanished. One reached for Trundle. "If he won't give me my cash back, I'll take it from you." He snatched at her tattered robe.

"She doesn't have any, numbskull," Mia hissed, pulling Trundle towards the exit. "Hannah!" she shouted. "We're leaving!"

Hannah was torn between trying to get the announcer to speak and getting Trundle to safety. She opted for the latter.

"We're going to shut this place down," she said.

"Oh, you can try, but we have friends in high places. Or since we're LineFolk, maybe that's low places."

She darted out the door, back to the auditorium, where she intercepted Mia and Trundle, who were fighting off the crowd. She opened her mouth to tell Mia who she had seen, then decided it could wait for a better moment.

"Hello Hannah," Trundle said, as though she had just bumped into her in the street. "I didn't expect to see you here either."

"Are you OK?" Hannah asked, poking and prodding at Trundle's body, looking for injuries.

"Yes, thank you. I feel very good. Are you OK?"

"I'm holding up, Trundle." She pulled her gently to the exit. "We are leaving."

Trundle resisted. "What about Pascal?" She looked back at the stage.

"He just tried to kill you!" Mia reminded her. "He can look after himself."

"He did," Trundle confirmed in her unique way. "But he didn't want to."

"There's no time," Mia said.

"Wait," Hannah interrupted. "This might be a chance for me to understand how I'm reversing a change. Maybe I'll be able to control it better." She jogged down to the stage where Pascal sat, forlorn.

"Come with me," she said over the bellow of the crowd. "We can keep you safe."

The ogre appeared doubtful.

"Do you speak English?" Hannah checked, remembering that Pascal had been brought from France. He nodded. "So, come. But if you do, it has to be now."

The ogre shuffled to the edge of the stage and hopped down. He looked at his hands and flexed them, as though still surprised that he was in human form again. Hannah took a hand and pulled him up the ramp, where Mia and Trundle waited. Pascal shot an embarrassed smile at the troll, snatched an abandoned coat from a seat, and then they ran.

***

Hannah fumbled for her phone. They were sheltering under the awning of a mini-market around the corner from the theatre. No one had followed them, as far as they knew. They weren't worth it. There were probably other fights to watch.

"Patel? It's me. We need a lift. No, I know you're not a *fucking* minicab. You're going to want to hear about this. Mia, me, Trundle, and a plus one. Yes, *that* Trundle. No, I don't think we're in danger, but we can't catch a bus, can we? Yeah, I know we could take the Tube, but Trundle's lost most of her clothes, and I'm pretty sure Pascal doesn't have a fucking Oyster card. Yeah, he's LineFolk. Sort of. Can you have foreign LineFolk? Does that make them OtherFolk?"

"Tell him to stop arguing and get over here," Mia said.

"You heard that? And will you? Thanks. We're outside Liverpool Street."

"There was a time he would have come running because you sneezed, darling."

"Not the moment for teasing me, Mia."

"I never could work out what his deal was. Is he on our side or not?"

"I don't think it matters. He is what he is. Generally helpful, even as a taxi service."

It was fifteen minutes before a people carrier pulled up outside the station and flashed its lights.

"Police cutbacks?" Hannah asked.

"It's my weekend with the kids," Patel muttered. "Luckily for you, Aditi is at a sleepover, and I don't need to get Arjun from nets yet. I assume you want to go to the clynic?"

Hannah nodded.

"It's not a simple route from here. Not with the other three in the car. I don't like the idea of ripped upholstery."

"I have never been in a car," Trundle announced.

"Follow the Central Line," Hannah said. "It runs under St Paul's, Newgate. And once you get to Tottenham Court Road, you know the safe way."

"You've done your research," Patel said in admiration. "Got the whole topography in your head?"

"Pretty much. It's an essential life skill these days."

Hannah held the doors open. The three LineFolk looked at the car as though it were on fire.

"It's safe," she insisted. "Patel knows the drill. He'll stick to a line all the way. Pascal, did you understand that? You'll stay human."

They slid into the rear seats, and Hannah stepped away. "Where are you going?" Patel asked. "Get in the car, and then I can get back to my evening."

"I need to speak to you in private. Before we go."

Patel leaned out the window and looked at the sky, which was threatening to dump a spring shower onto the city, then sighed and got out.

Hannah led him from the car towards the station.

"I saw Tarrin."

"Where?"

"Here. Well, over there. Did you know there is some sort of sick LineFolk cage fighting happening in an old theatre over the road?"

Patel looked across the street. "There's a City of London police station over there."

"Yeah, it's right under their noses." Hannah leaned in. "In fact, I think someone there might know about it. One of the LineFolk over there mentioned a cop."

"It doesn't sound illegal," Patel said, seemingly not that interested in the activity and itching to get the conversation back to Tarrin. "Although if that man's involved, it's probably shady."

"Not illegal? They are making LineFolk fight to the death. It's desperate."

"And you were there because...?"

"Because one of the survivors turned up on our doorstep."

"Hannah, if you keep following up on every sob story that enters number fifty, you won't have any time left for actually treating them."

"Compassionate as ever, I see."

He shrugged. "Just battle-hardened, I guess. And yeah, it's not illegal because there are no laws that I could use to stop LineFolk from doing anything. How am I supposed to pass a file to the CPS that says, 'mythical beasts did it'?"

Tap, tap, tap.

"Oh, what now?!" Hannah screamed.

Patel held up his hands. "Bit extreme..."

"Not you," she snapped. "The tapping. Tell me that you can hear that."

"Nothing, sorry."

Knock, tap, tap.

"Really, you didn't hear the knocking?"

"Let's drive you all back," Patel said. "I'll get someone to pick up Arjun for me, and we can talk about Tarrin and whatever he's up to."

"Did you know that's the first time you've told me your kids' names?"

"No, I suppose they never came up before."

Tap, tap, tap.

Was it sounding more insistent?

Hannah stared at the station entrance. The noise wasn't coming from there. In fact, it wasn't coming from anywhere in particular. It just...was.

"I think I need to get my ears checked," she muttered. "Come on, let's head out of here."

Chapter 11

FLYNN WAS ECSTATIC TO have Mia safely back, but less pleased to find Patel and an unfamiliar man in the clynic as well.

"We have to think about the cubs," he whispered. "First the selkie and now this...Frenchman."

Hannah noted that Flynn seemed as xenophobic about the French as many of his human counterparts often were.

After Mia had checked on the children, Hannah pulled her aside. "There's no easy way to tell you this." She fiddled nervously with her sleeves, uncharacteristically ill at ease. "I saw your father."

"What? Where? At the theatre?"

Hannah nodded. "In the shadows, but I'm sure it was him."

"So, you can't be certain then," Mia insisted, clinging to the uncertainty. "There was a lot going on."

"I know it was him, Mi. He was watching. He almost certainly spotted you."

"If he had been there and seen me, he would have let me know he was there."

"If he wanted to let you know he was around, he could have done it at any point in the last three months. Written a letter, or sent a messenger."

Mia shook her head. "No, he will be missing his grandchildren, even if he doesn't really want to see me. He wouldn't have spurned an opportunity like that to make contact, not with me in front of him."

"Of course he would. He was watching real-life gladiators in a London building. And worse. He was bankrolling it."

Mia locked eyes with Hannah, and the gaze returned was unflinching.

"OK, so I have a lot to learn about my father, but the situation with the swerves was incompetent over-ambition. What we watched tonight was pure evil."

"I understand why you wouldn't want to contemplate his involvement, but you have to admit that it's a possibility."

"I need more than you catching a glimpse of someone who *might* have been Daddy," Mia said determinedly.

In a stand-off the two women joined the others, clustered in the drawing room, Pascal and Ruadh sitting uncomfortably on the sofa while the rest perched on chair arms and coffee tables.

"There is no word on the street about the cage?" Hannah asked Patel.

"Nothing," the detective said. "And it's hard to understand how it's remained a secret. How long has it been going on?"

"I think I can answer that," Flynn suggested, ceasing his pacing for a moment. "The reports of the headless lady's return started three weeks ago. So that's three weeks since the pit began fuelling phantasms with LineFolk misery once again."

"But there is no 'pit' there," Mia insisted. "It's an old dweller theatre, with a rudimentary cage-fighting setup."

"The theatre you described may not have been a cockfighting pit, but there was one nearby. On Cock Hill, to the east. I imagine that's where the street name came from. The pits were all connected through human-cruelty, whether it was birds or LineFolk who died in them. If the one near Liverpool Street is active once more, it will have energised all the old sites beside the Ouroborus. Cockpit Steps is very close to the Ouroborus. It's been active for three weeks."

"Trundle," Hannah asked. "Was there fighting every day? How many bouts?"

"I was only there for twenty-four hours, but there was a fight every thirty minutes."

"So there could have been hundreds of LineFolk deaths already. Enough to reboot a phantasm?"

"It's supposition, but yes," Flynn nodded.

Hannah turned to Ruadh. "It's time for your story. We know where you were. We saw it with our own eyes. And we know you were forced to fight a werecat. We don't know why, though."

Ruadh still didn't look keen to share.

"OK," Hannah sighed. "I'll cut straight to the point. Does Ethelred Tarrin have your pelt? Is he the one holding you in bondage in human form? Is he your entwined?"

Flynn's jaw dropped so far it nearly hit the fireplace.

"Hannah," Mia exclaimed. "Now you are just making things up."

Ruadh looked around the room. "No, she's not. Mr Tarrin has my skin. I am bound to him," she sighed wearily. "He seemed so compassionate when we met him. When we first came to London, he found work for my father."

"When was that?" Hannah asked.

"Fifteen years ago, when I was very young. My father and I left the ocean and travelled south. We were driven from our homelands by construction on our beaches. He rolled up my pelt and packed it away for the time when we would return to the sea. But it was hard here.

We aren't dwellers, and we're not really LineFolk, but something in between. We couldn't live as humans, and the LineFolk didn't want us either."

"You seem very human to me," Hannah comforted her.

Ruadh didn't appear to appreciate the observation. "Years of living with the worms helps you to blend in. But it was different back then. We had been around the fringes of humankind before, but only in remote areas. Can you imagine what it was like seeing a skyscraper or a supermarket for the first time?"

"No," Hannah admitted.

"Mr Tarrin offered help. He said that we shouldn't risk having our pelts with us because the city wasn't safe. He took them and locked them away. And helped my father find employment."

Hannah marvelled inwardly at how Ruadh's story mirrored that of the cyoeraeth Tafs and her brother. Tarrin seemed to hoover up the strays of the LineFolk world, if he thought they might serve a purpose.

"And now you can't return to the sea because he has never returned your skins."

Ruadh nodded her head.

"I don't understand how that resulted in your being in a fighting cage?" Mia said, a little too aggressively for Hannah's liking.

"My father has something Mr Tarrin wants."

"Sounds like a potential exchange to me," Hannah suggested. "Your pelts for whatever it is he needs from your father."

"We've found that Mr Tarrin doesn't strike deals. He just takes what he desires."

Hannah glanced at Mia, but she was staring wide-eyed at her husband.

"So he put you in the cage to persuade your father to give it up?"

Ruadh shrugged.

"And you called his bluff—went in there, regardless."

"It's not like that. It wasn't a bluff. I told Father not to back down. If I died, then Tarrin wouldn't have any hold over him."

"You went there expecting to die?" Hannah asked, disbelieving.

"Being in this concrete hellhole is worse than death."

"But you came here," Hannah reminded her. "You must have been close to death, but you struggled to the clynic for help."

"I realised, lying in the street outside Grubb's, that if Mr Tarrin would actually let me die, he would never release my father from his bondage. He would just find another way to get him to comply. And so I decided to live, because I'm no use dead. But Father mustn't know, or Mr Tarrin. While they think I'm gone, maybe the pressure will be off."

"Don't you want your father to know you're alive?"

"Of course I do, but not at the expense of Mr Tarrin having something to blackmail him with again."

Mia, who had been pacing by the fireplace, abruptly interjected.

"Alright, if my father is this demon that you describe, what does he want from *your* father? What's so precious that your father would let you die to keep it?"

"He's your father?" Ruadh gasped, pressing herself back into the sofa. Her eyes darted to the stairs. "No, no. I have to go."

Hannah put a hand across her lap. "It's OK. Mia and her father are not...aligned."

"She's a Tarrin," Ruadh spat. "Rich. Entitled. Manipulative."

"Yes," Mia agreed. "All of that. And I'm also one of the LineFolk who stopped him from creating a bloodbath on London's streets last year. So stop tarring me with his brush."

Ruadh settled into silence, but kept her eyes firmly on the were-cat.

"Your father," Hannah reminded her. "What does he have?"

"I don't know," she admitted. "He's not a wealthy man. He doesn't have precious things. All he cares about is his kin and the sea." She put a hand to her head. "I need to lie down."

Hannah didn't know if this was genuine or an attempt to avoid the questions, but there seemed little point in persisting. "You can have my room tonight," she said, trying hard not to look at Flynn and Mia, who were not happy with the waifs and strays in their house.

A bell rang from the landing.

"Excellent!" Flynn exclaimed, his mood visibly lifting. He exited in a haste that Hannah would have described as unseemly.

"Expecting a takeaway?" she snapped.

"That was not the doorbell," he replied redundantly. "I have a message."

"You've discovered technology?"

"Of course I haven't, although the messaging system is rather innovative. I'm going to the roof. Come see."

Anticipating a rusting contraption of semaphore flags, Hannah followed Flynn up two flights of stairs to the very top of the house, beyond even where the werecat and his wife had their rooms. She rarely had cause to come this far, just the occasional visit to look after the children, and was surprised to see a wooden ladder descending from the ceiling. It was disappearing into a hole from which a strong draft flooded the landing with cold air.

"Don't you care about our heating bills?" she asked.

Flynn quickly shimmied up, demonstrating the cat-like agility that bled into his human form. He gestured for her to follow, and she climbed up a little less confidently. There was a door at the top, open to the elements. A fine mist condensed on the doorframe.

"Is this where you've been spending so much time?" she called.

"Yes, there was a large backlog to work through. The Master never told me about this. I always assumed he was using a special power to get summoned to house visits, but it was a lot more mundane."

"We are thirty metres up on the roof," Hannah pointed out, looking at the felting, a forest of ventilation ducts, and the London skyline behind them. "This is not at all mundane."

"Well, yes, but that's not everything," he laughed. "There is something wonderful up here."

Flynn led her around a chimney stack, and a fantastic feathered sight greeted them—row after row of vibrant green birds, lined up on a pole strung across the roof. They huddled together in the cool of the night, gently shuffling their feet and grooming themselves happily. One bird was sitting apart from the others on a distinct perch. It too was grooming, but occasionally stopped to tap a paddle. Hannah could hear a faint ringing from below every time it tapped.

"Oh, Axton," Hannah said. "They're beautiful."

It was the first truly pretty sight she had encountered since discovering the LineFolk.

"London parakeets," Flynn purred. "At least, that's what the dwellers call them. We refer to them as carriers. They deliver messages between locations of interest to the LineFolk."

"You've trained them?" Hannah asked.

"Not at all. They seem to be driven to it. My elder-memories tell me that originally there were just about a dozen at a time flying in secret over London for centuries. A network of messenger birds that kept us connected, informed, and aligned. At some point in the 1960s, someone lost control of their flock. They fled, bred, and now there are thousands across London. It's as though the LineFolk have painted a giant billboard advertising their existence, but none of the dwellers have noticed. They've made up other myths to account for it."

"They're like pigeons, but beautiful ones. How does it work?"

Flynn didn't answer immediately. "I'm not entirely sure why the Master never told me about this. It suggests something worth keeping under wraps. I trust you completely with the secret of its existence, but I am wondering if the secret of how it works should remain just that."

"Bollocks to that, Axton." She walked up to the lone parakeet. It peered at her with the side of its head and offered its foot. There was a band around its leg. Hannah looked back at Flynn.

"Go on," he said. "You may as well now you've decided to break with centuries of tradition."

"A tradition you knew nothing about until a couple of months ago." Hannah gingerly took hold of the parakeet's foot. It didn't seem at all bothered. In fact, it was encouraging her to remove the band. It had a hinge and catch which popped apart easily under pressure. One half of the band was hollow, and a tiny scroll had been slid inside, tightly rolled. She pulled it out, and it unravelled of its own accord. There was a dense collection of symbols written on one side—small lines adorning longer lines that ran the length of the paper.

"What is this?" Hannah asked, showing the page to Flynn, who patted the parakeet on the head before it stretched its wings and fluttered to join its companions on the other perch. "Is it Morse code?"

"Not dissimilar," Flynn said, taking the note from her. "It's ogham. An ancient writing method from the far reaches of Albion and Ériu. It was used solely for Old Irish, or Gallic, but phonetically it can be applied to English...at a push. Which is useful, because I have many memories lurking in my brain, but how to speak Celtic languages is one that would require a lot of retrieval and processing."

"Why is there a parakeet carrying a message in..."

"Ogham."

"...ogham, on our roof? Is this why you've been spending so much time up here recently?"

"Yes, I'm like a child with a new toy. You have your telephone, I have my birds. They deliver messages from all across the Ouroborus. I admit that only the upper echelons of LineFolk society have access, but those are the customers that keep us going, so it's important for me to stay on top of their needs."

Hannah noted that this was the first time Flynn had ever referenced the economics of the practice, and she resolved to bring it up again another day.

"You can read that?"

Flynn squinted at the scratchings on the page. "Yes, although I wish it could be bigger, and I also wish I had those reading glasses with me that you were mocking earlier this week. This request is for a house visit tomorrow to an unwell pixie in the Mary's Bone safezone, so not far from here at all. I'll reply in the affirmative."

He flipped the paper over and scribbled what appeared to be a haphazard set of lines, then looked at the birds lined up watching him. One, seemingly at random, fluttered over to the single perch where it offered its leg. Although they were all identical, Hannah was sure it wasn't the same parakeet as had delivered the message.

"How does it know where to go?"

Flynn smiled. "Oh, that's a rather interesting and amazing feat. Requesting a destination is fairly simple, but how these Amazonian avians can interpret that and fly unerringly to one of hundreds of destinations around London remains a mystery to me. They just seem to know."

He reached into a tiny cupboard at the base of the perch and extracted a small book. He flicked through until he found the page he was looking for and showed Hannah. A pattern formed of nine squares in a three-by-three grid. Each square was either black or white.

"This is the address for the patient. I just show this to the bird and it knows where to go. But first, I have to make sure the message is in the band. I haven't risked seeing what happens if you offer them the address before securing it. They might fly off too soon."

"Each location has its own pattern?"

"Yes, there are 512 possibilities, and therefore 512 addresses. This is us!"

Flynn flicked the book around and showed Hannah the grid. It was a simple pattern with only a single square blacked out—in the centre.

"That design's very basic. It's hard to imagine that whoever created this system wasn't here, at the clynic," Hannah observed.

Flynn pursed his lips. "True, I had never considered that. If so, then I really must spend more time trawling through the memory banks." He rapped the side of his head with his knuckles and rolled the reply into a tiny tube, sliding it into a band that he clipped onto the parakeet earmarked for the return. He then flicked through the book until he found the patient's address and spun it around so the bird could examine it intently. With minimal fuss, it spread its wings and took flight, rapidly heading north at roof height up the centre of the road.

"Is Tarrin's address in there?" Hannah asked.

"Yes, why do you ask?"

"Could Mia use a bird to make contact? Less threatening than a face-to-face meeting. Less dangerous as well."

"In theory, although I think she is very conflicted right now. Please don't suggest it."

"I won't," Hannah promised, but it was hard to take her mind off the thaumatagineer. She knew that she hadn't seen the last of Tarrin when he disappeared from Golden Square all those months ago, but he had reappeared in the most unlikely of circumstances, and that couldn't be good.

Chapter 12

WHEN HER WATCH BUZZED with a new message, it caught Hannah by surprise. She only had a second to glance at it as she was busy holding down a very uncooperative patient.

Dinner?

"Who's asking you out?" Flynn asked, catlike curiosity compelling him to look at her wrist as he struggled to get a grip on the splinter in the werecat's paw while it thrashed unhelpfully. "Believe me, I know it's tough to control yourself in this form," he said pointedly at the writhing feline, "but this will all be over much more quickly if you can let more human instincts have some agency."

He was calling it a splinter, but Hannah felt that was not doing justice to the size of the piece of wood sticking into the soft flesh between the cat's paw pads. The patient had arrived in human form, of course, and Flynn had suggested he move into the no-go part of the consulting room, in the belief that the change would reject the foreign body and they could call the job done. This had turned out to be a false hope as the splinter, if anything, went further into the paw, protruding from the top. It was as long and as thick as a pencil. Now, the cat stretched his arm back into the safezone where Flynn could safely work. His limb writhed as though unsure whether it was trying to be human or feline.

She tried to look at her watch again, but the screen had turned off. "Not sure. I haven't met anyone who would ask me to dinner. Mia maybe?"

"You live in the same house," Flynn pointed out. "And just because she gives in to her human side and carries a phone with her, it doesn't mean she is lazy enough to use it to communicate with you."

The cat hissed at them both, its speech passably recognisable. "Stop talking about her date and get it out."

"I don't think it's a date," Hannah insisted, but the cat roared, and she felt it was best to focus on the task in front of her. "Mr Flynn, have you considered softening the skin first? Maybe a warm bath for the affected hand."

Flynn looked at her curiously. "No, we'll just go for a surprise removal."

"How will it be a surprise if I kno...argggh." The cat roared again as Flynn deftly slid the splinter out and rapidly covered the wound with a cloth. "Please apply pressure, Nurse Chadwick," he suggested, tossing the piece of wood into a bowl.

"I saw Julius do that so many times, I lost count," he said. "Always try to catch them out. You'll be fine, Heckworth," he told the patient. "It's a clean entry and exit, and I don't believe it requires stitches. The nurse will dress it, but I think you need to limit the use of the hand for a couple of weeks. In fact, if you make your way over here to the sofa, you may find the change to human form does most of the hard work for you."

While Heckworth relaxed back into his disguise, Hannah checked her phone.

The messenger had been persistent.

You there?

Sorry, is this odd?

It was from Patel.

She wasn't sure how she felt about the police officer asking her out. He was obviously fond of her, and she had a lot to thank him for, but maybe that was all it was.

Still, dinner couldn't hurt, could it?

She tried to lighten the mood.

I only go for dinner with people who tell me their first name

She waited nervously for the reply.

detective sergeant. I'll tell you for real if you come for dinner

"Nurse Chadwick, could you please find Heckworth's shirt? This room feels much colder than usual." Flynn attempted to peer over her shoulder at her phone, and she shifted her body to block his view.

"No secret, it's Patel," she told him.

"Oh." Flynn looked a bit put out. "I was hoping for some intrigue. One could already tell he had a soft spot for you."

"You could?" Hannah asked, a little surprised. As far as she knew, the couple of times that Patel had shown her, through a slight touch or taking her hand, that he liked her, they had been on their own.

"Of course, you could. Mia says it's 'one-way chemistry' though."

"I don't want to lead him on."

"So, don't go to dinner."

"Well, I think I'd like to. The only time I leave this building is when there's a crisis."

Deal. Where?

"You just said yes, didn't you?" Flynn scoffed. "I can tell by your smile."

"Excuse me," Heckworth interrupted. "I really want my shirt back."

***

Flynn and Mia stood at the door like worried parents as she left number fifty. Hannah wasn't sure if they were concerned or fishing for gossip. Mia picked lint off her coat in the manner of a mother cat grooming a kitten.

Patel had suggested they meet at a Lebanese restaurant near Baker Street. Hannah must have walked past it a dozen times, but London was awash with great places to eat, and this one had never caught her eye. He was hovering outside as she approached, wearing his trademark leather jacket. She surprised herself by being disappointed that he hadn't made an effort, and immediately felt self-conscious that she had fished out the only nice dress from the suitcase she'd been living out of for two months.

"Hey," Patel said nonchalantly and smiled in an unconvincing way, as if he were trying out an expression he wasn't used to showing off.

"Remember the deal," Hannah said. "I don't have dinner with people whose first names I don't know. As much as I think Patel suits you, I'm not calling you that all night."

"Won't you let me keep any secrets?"

She glared at him in jest until he crumbled.

"It's Shiv."

"Nice to meet you, Shiv," Hannah said, shaking his hand with formality. "Was that so hard?"

"TV detectives never have first names," he said grumpily. "It makes them more mysterious."

"There is enough mystery in our lives without adding to it by keeping that information from each other. If you play your cards right, I might tell you my middle names before the night is over."

"Names?" Patel checked. "Do you have more than one?"

"I think my parents were indecisive." They lapsed into an awkward silence. "Are we going inside?" Hannah asked.

"Yes, yes," Patel said, snapping out of his nervous paralysis.

They sat at a table for two, sandwiched tightly between other couples. Hannah was sure her elbows were brushing against their neighbours, such was the proximity. She realised that, far from being a problem, this meant that the conversation would have to steer well clear of the LineFolk. For a couple of hours, she had to think and talk about normal things.

"Where are the kids tonight?" she asked.

"With their mother for the next few days, then I'll get Aditi back. Arjun has an inset day." Patel replied. It felt uncomfortable to be reminded immediately that Patel had an ex-wife, but, come to think of it, he never referred to her that way. She glanced at his hands. No wedding ring, although that wasn't a cast-iron sign.

He saw her looking at his finger and held it up in front of her. "Look, not even a mark. I haven't worn it in five years."

Hannah looked away, embarrassed. "Sorry, but I'm intrigued. And I don't want to get myself into something that I regret."

"This is just dinner," he reassured her. "Friends."

"Yes, friends."

They stared at their menus for a minute, but there was too much choice for Hannah's liking, and none of the options tempted her. She was relieved when the waiter came over for the drinks order, and Patel picked a wine. "How about we get a sharing platter?" he suggested, sensing her indecision.

"That sounds great," she said, pleased to switch off her brain. "Do you come here often? Sorry, that's so cliched, but you know what I mean."

"Not often, but I've been here before. It's on the Ouroborus though, so I always feel a bit exposed."

Hannah raised her eyebrows at him and cocked her head at their neighbours. He got the message and went back to studying the menu.

"Do you ever feel lonely?" Hannah blurted out. "Knowing what you know, but not having anyone to speak to about it?"

"I have my boss," Patel shrugged. "But yes, I feel lonely. It's OK though, I don't need anyone."

"That is exactly what I would expect someone to say if they really needed someone."

Patel gave a half-smile. "Yeah, well, I have you now."

Hannah smiled back. "Yes, you do."

The meal passed pleasantly. They talked about growing up—Patel in west London, and Hannah in the leafy Surrey town of Redhill. They had both felt a calling to their professions from a young age, and Patel had joined the Police Service straight out of university, but Hannah had taken a while to decide what she wanted before committing to nursing. Her parents had wished for something different, and she wasted years trying to work out how to satisfy their ambitions for her, when she didn't share those dreams.

"Do you think your parents might know more than they let on?" Patel asked as the evening moved on and their closest neighbours finished up and paid, affording them some privacy. "Because you are obviously special."

"About the LineFolk? No!"

"I wondered if that's why they steered you away from being a nurse."

"No, they were just snobbish. I mean, I probably could have done something that satisfied their vision for me."

"Were?"

"Yes, they're dead. So I can't go back and interrogate them."

"Someone in your family tree knew for sure."

Hannah nodded. "One day I'll find out. What about you, Shiv? You've hinted about a connection to the LineFolk yourself."

"Yeah, I've been around them for a while."

"What's your origin story? When did you discover them?"

Patel sat back in his chair as though preparing for a long tale. "It was about seven years ago. I was a DC at the time and very much learning the ropes, but—and you'll find this very hard to believe, I'm sure—I was a bit of a dick, and my boss gave me a dead end case to investigate."

"Not so dead end in the...end?"

"Definitely not a dead end. Have you heard of the Kennington Loop?"

"I've heard of Kennington..."

Patel raised an eyebrow. "Well, it is south of the river, and I get the feeling you're a North London girl. And way outside the Ouroborus, so it's probably dead to you now. Anyway, the loop is where the southbound Northern line trains terminate, then travel on an extended underground path that returns them to the northbound platform."

Hannah grinned. "A few months ago, if someone had talked about underground railway routes on a date, I would have bailed straight away, but why do I think that there's something interesting about to happen in this story?"

"Date?" Patel said slowly.

"Is that not what this is? Friends or otherwise."

He didn't answer. "There were reports of really odd things happening on the trains that ran the loop. Drivers were hearing chatter in carriages that were supposed to be completely empty. The occasional passenger who fell asleep and rode the loop by mistake came back with stories of weird, incomprehensible announcements, flickering lights, and slamming doors."

"Ooh," Hannah said, trying to ignore the hanging question about the date. "Spooky."

"Yeah, very. It became so frequent that they sent the police down to investigate. Well, really it was just keeping the unions happy by pretending to, which is why they dispatched me. The newest, greenest, most naive detective available. I sat on those bloody trains riding that loop again, and again, and again, for days on end. I'd get on at Kennington—southbound platform—then get off on the northbound platform and take the stairs back to the southbound. For ever and ever until I went completely insane."

"Did you see anything?"

"I saw a lot of things. Mostly dirty train carriages, the same advertisements over and over, and once in a while, a drunk person to break the monotony."

"No ghosts?"

"No ghosts, which is ironic, because a few days later it all changed for me. I begged the Chief to pull me off the job. She told me it was good for me to follow orders, and that she sent all the chippy recruits on the loop until they broke."

Hannah smiled. "You are chippy. So, she didn't really expect you to see anything paranormal."

"Nah, of course not. She assumed it was all just overactive imagination. But my boast is that I lasted for six days, and that beat the record by a whole four, so I was in her good books. She called me back to HQ, and I couldn't get there quickly enough. I was on the southbound platform at the time, and I thought that rather than use the stairs to get to the northbound, I'd take one last trip on the loop."

Hannah could tell where this was going. "You saw something."

Patel smiled. "Oh yeah. I sure did. I'd spent six days staring at the carriage walls, waiting for something to happen inside the train. I got to know the drivers, so I knocked on the window and asked if I could ride in the cab. I mean, I'm a cop, right? So they couldn't say no. Those guys must have ridden that loop a thousand times. He wasn't even looking out the windscreen. But I was. And I saw them darting into alcoves in the wall as the train approached. Clinging to the roof of the tunnel. Weird, pale creatures. Hairless."

"What were they?"

Patel shook his head. "I don't know to this day. I'm actually a little scared to find out. It's outside the Ouroborus, so they aren't hiding in plain sight. They are just hiding. I told the driver what I'd seen, and he laughed. He told me it was because I was looking for something strange on the loop. I knew I wasn't seeing things. I rode that train all the way back to Charing Cross, thinking about them. And from that moment onwards, I opened my eyes. Watched everything. I didn't ignore the weird shit I saw at midnight on a quiet station. I sat at the entrance to the platforms, checking out the weirdos sucking in what I now know is linether."

"But that's just watching. There are weirdos all over the Tube, and most of them aren't LineFolk."

Patel sighed. "Yeah. That was when I came across Flora." But then he went silent.

"Tell me more," Hannah said.

"Sorry, Hannah. I'm not ready to talk about that."

She felt unreasonably put out. They shared so much, and this was just a story that would help her understand. Patel could see her irritation.

"I know that's annoying, but it's no reflection on you that I'm not talking about it."

"I think it is. You said earlier that it's nice to have me to talk to. And this sounds as though it's something you need to talk about."

It was Patel's turn to be irritated. "You have no idea what you're saying. And it's none of your business."

She didn't want the night to end on a sour note. "I'm sorry, Shiv. I shouldn't have pressed you. Let's settle up the bill and call it a day."

Patel gestured at the waiter, and they sat in silence for a minute. He reached for a card from his wallet and dropped it on the table.

"Split it," Hannah suggested, but he didn't look keen.

"I've still got my manners."

Knock, knock, knock.

This time it was accompanied by a stabbing pain in her temples. She put her head in her hands and grimaced.

"Come on," Patel sighed. "Don't be dramatic. It's just something I'm not willing to talk about. One day I will."

"It's not about you," Hannah groaned. "It's my head. Agony. The knocking is back."

Patel looked around the restaurant. "There's nothing here."

Tap, TAP, TAAAP.

"Please get me out of here."

He helped her up and into her coat. They stumbled into the street, arm in arm, and Hannah gulped in the cold air. The knocking sound swirled around her, coming from everywhere at once. The pain came and went, but never altogether, and the urgency of the beat was tangible.

"I can't bear it. We've got to make it stop."

"I don't know how," Patel said desperately. "We really must get you to Flynn. Somewhere in that encyclopaedia he calls a brain, there has to be an answer."

"The answer isn't in Flynn's head. It's in the tunnels. I can feel it. Something wants me down there."

"Did you not hear my story just now? There are monsters in the tunnels, not solutions."

Hannah looked at the entrance to Baker Street station a few yards away. "Take me there. Maybe I will know what to do if I'm closer."

Chapter 13

PATEL FLASHED A BADGE at the gate attendant, who swiped the barriers open. "She's with me," he said and encouraged Hannah through. "Can you get a sense of direction yet?"

"No, it's everywhere," she moaned. "It's as if the knocking is inside my head."

There was no point in calling out the attacks as they happened. The rhythm had become constant and reverberated in her skull with the steady cadence of a heartbeat. The tone was metallic, like two iron bars being banged together repeatedly.

"Let's go down," Hannah suggested. "I don't know why, but the noise feels...deep."

"Can you use the...you know?" Patel asked.

"The linether? I have no idea what I can and can't do. But this doesn't feel connected. Honestly, I think it's more likely I'm going insane."

They hopped onto the escalator descending to the Bakerloo and Jubilee lines. Patel walked briskly on the left, too impatient to stand, pushing past the out-of-towners who were unaware of the convention of always standing on the right. By the time Hannah reached the bottom, he had been waiting there for ten seconds.

There was a busker in the lobby, playing a mournful tune on a clarinet that echoed throughout the tunnels. Hannah knew immediately he was LineFolk. The linether created an intentional aura about him that was distinct from the way it parted around the dwellers. It danced with the music in a manner she had never seen before, interacting with the rhythm. The musician looked at Hannah without missing a beat of the song and cocked his head slightly. LineFolk needed to touch each other to know for sure, but Hannah must have been lit up like a beacon.

Patel spotted Hannah's distraction and followed her gaze to the busker. "Him?" he asked.

"No, he's regular LineFolk. I was just...experimenting."

"The knocking?"

"Still there. Let's go onto the platform."

The lobby filled with the hot gust of an approaching train, and Hannah pushed into it, closing her eyes as tunnel grit spiralled in the air.

The train disgorged its passengers, and suddenly they were heading against a torrent of humanity, aiming for the escalators. Momentarily, Hannah forgot the knocking as she was buffeted from side to side, losing her balance and stumbling. Then Patel wrapped an arm around her, holding the other out—a ramrod-straight battering ram. The crowd parted like the Red Sea on either side of them.

"Thanks," Hannah whispered. Patel smiled faintly, and she felt him hold her a little tighter. He waited, standing firm until all but the stragglers had passed.

"We can come back another time," he said.

"No, I can't bear this noise in my head. I want it to stop."

Patel took her hand, and they walked onto the platform as the train exited, howling into the southbound tunnel. The scream ebbed and flowed in pitch—higher, lower, higher, lower—and the tracks rattled with a frenzied vibration. As it disappeared, the screaming continued, but to Hannah's horror, it was no longer coming from the train, but instead sat in her head like an electric drill. It too ebbed and flowed, but the screams were distinct.

Lord, save us.

Sweet Jesus.

My arm, my arm!

"The tracks," she gasped. "Are they rattling?"

Patel felt her slump into one of the plastic benches against the wall.

"No, nothing."

"I can hear rattling. It's like there's a train coming into the platform, only out of control."

"I promise you, Hannah, the platform is empty."

The screaming built to a crescendo in her head, and she clamped hands over her ears, but it served only to focus the noise.

"Make it stop!" she screamed.

And it did.

She felt a hand brush across her back, and she jumped. Patel yelped as he experienced something similar. "Someone tried to grab my handcuffs!" He spun on the spot, his leather jacket flaring, revealing for a moment his equipment hidden in the pockets.

Hannah heard giggling, and the hand brushed her arm. She sensed it reaching into the pocket of her coat, and she slapped at it, but only disturbed thin air.

"Stop that, Pip," said a voice in her ear.

Hannah snapped her head around. There was no one there.

"Sorry," the voice added.

"Who's there?" she asked, frustrated.

"My old name was John Puddle." The tone was soft, young, with an archaic West Country burr that was out of place in the London Underground.

Hannah felt happier with the sudden appearance of a dialogue.

"OK, John Puddle. Why is your voice in my head?"

"Tha' I don't quite know, ma'am."

"You're the one putting it there. What do you mean, you don't know?"

"Oftentimes I try to speak to those wha' we are warning, but they never talk back. They can just hear the knocking. You's the first."

Patel was looking at Hannah as though she were mad. He gave her an inquisitive thumbs-up, and she replied with a so-so gesture and tapped her ear. He shook his head in disbelief, but he had seen enough in recent times not to question whether what was happening was real or not, and wandered off down the platform poking at fixtures and fittings, and occasionally tapping on a wall.

"And you are trying to warn me, are you, John Puddle?"

"Yes, ma'am. We are."

"We?"

"Yes, ma'am. Me and the others. We are all here. Apart from Elias and Davey Johnson. They are a few yards away. They died early, you see, so we can never be completely together."

Hannah immediately picked up on the word 'died'.

"You're a ghost?"

"We don't like that term, ma'am. Would you be amenable to coming into our chamber so we's able to explain?"

"You can't just tell me here?"

"I could, I s'pose, but the platform will fill up soon, and then you would be talking to yourself, an' I suspect you would prefer some privacy. I proper don't want to have to rush. You's the first mortal person I've spoken to in almost ten score years."

"OK," Hannah agreed. "Where is your chamber?"

"Up the stairs behind you, take a left, and there's a door there. Made from dark wood, and a rare sight because of all the decorations on there. Michael says they are signs, but I can't read like he can, so to me I just enjoy the pictures."

"What's on the other side of the door?"

"We are, ma'am, and the baffles, and the shaft. It's easier if we show you."

Hannah had to admit to herself that she was enjoying being called ma'am. If politeness were a measure of trustworthiness, then John Puddle was a diamond.

"We're moving," she told Patel. "We are cordially invited to meet the tappers."

"Knockers, ma'am."

"Sorry?"

"Knockers. We are known as the Knockers, not the Tappers."

"Bully for you," Hannah said, then instantly regretted the sarcasm. She had been driven to distraction by the knocking noise, and now the disarming voice that claimed responsibility was soothing her righteous anger. This in itself was disconcertingly irritating.

"Where are we moving to?" Patel asked, confused about who was speaking to whom.

Hannah took his hand, the first time she had initiated it, and led him up the stairs and to the left. As John Puddle had said, there was a door, varnished plywood, and covered in health and safety signs. It was not a work of art, despite what the Knocker suggested. There was no handle, only a keyhole. She pushed it gently, and the frame flexed a little, but it was locked.

"Are you still there, John?" she whispered. The sound of the clarinet was reverberating from the escalator lobby, and her whisper was practically a whisper-shout.

"Yes, ma'am. We are waiting. You just need to open the door."

"It's locked."

John Puddle was silent.

Hannah turned to Patel. "Can you open it? Do you have a special Tube key or something?"

"I don't have a *special Tube key*, but I have a shoulder." Patel leaned hard on the door, and the frame bent inwards. He pulled away. "It will go, but are you sure? I should really just ask someone to let us in."

"Don't be asking anyone else for help, ma'am," the Knocker insisted. "We's picked this spot because they usually never look here."

"No," Hannah said. "We don't have time."

Patel shrugged, stepped back a pace, then thrust himself at the door. It was nothing like the films. Rather than the frame splintering dramatically and the door banging open, the catch just popped gently. He smiled smugly at Hannah, who applauded.

She pushed the door tentatively, and it opened onto a pitch-black corridor that smelt damp and neglected. Patel flicked on a torch, and the beam was sharp, illuminating floating dust particles.

He cast the torchlight around the walls and found a metal switch, which had probably been there for fifty years. When toggled, there was the hum of fluorescent starters igniting, and harsh white light flickered on in sections.

"What are we looking for?" Patel asked.

"I don't know, but look at this place!"

The door had opened into a low-ceilinged room. The walls were lined with cream tiles, interspersed with peeling posters from a bygone era. It had, at some point, been a part of the station accessed by passengers, but was now sealed off. The floor was concrete and crumbling. They chose their steps carefully as they moved into the hidden area, which expanded out into a cavernous space, fifty metres high, heading into the open air on the surface. An abandoned lift shaft.

"John?" Hannah whispered. "Are you there?"

Giggles echoed around the room, but Patel didn't react. He still couldn't hear it.

"Ow!" Something pulled Hannah's hair.

"Pip, stop yer meddling," an older voice scolded, but more distant.

"Yes, Pa," laughed a youthful voice.

"You say she can hear us?" the older voice asked.

"Yes, Michael. The lady can hear us as clear as you could hear your Pammy when she called you for supper."

"Can we see you?" Hannah asked.

"People can't do that, ma'am."

"I'm not people though. I can hear you, and you said that wasn't normal. Are you standing in a particular place?"

"Right in front of you, ma'am."

Hannah couldn't help jumping, despite there being nothing there.

"An' Michael is here as well, an' if he ever stops playing, Pip could be here an' all."

She squinted. The particles of dust floating in the beam were swirling chaotically, but there was a space in front of her where they diverted, as though repelled by an invisible force. She remembered the headless lady and the spray that Flynn had given her. If she closed her eyes, she could see the linether just as clearly. Here at Baker Street, the atmosphere was thick with it. She pushed it gently towards the patch of air with no dust, and the linether wrapped itself around a shape—an obviously human form.

"I can see you, John. Sort of. I can see where you are anyway. Move your arms."

The dust and the linether swirled accordingly as John created patterns in the air.

"Is this room special to you? You seem to move around the station."

"We can move, ma'am. But this is where we feel safe. We're able to interact with things you understand, and it's easy to be spotted out there."

"I felt you touch me."

"Not me, ma'am. That was young Pip, although he's not much younger than me, to be truthful."

"You should call me Hannah. No need to be so formal."

"Yes, ma'am."

She decided not to labour the request. "So why have you brought us here, John?"

"To warn you, ma'am. Something dreadful is going to happen in the tunnels."

"And you know this how?"

"We just know, ma'am. We always know when something bad is coming where men have dug to hell itself."

"This is the Jubilee Line, John. Not hell."

"Tunnelling is always hell, ma'am. An' proper dangerous work with it. Just look at us."

"What happened to you?"

"We died, ma'am. At ol' Saltilack."

"I'm sorry, John. I don't know what that is."

The Knocker went silent as though processing Hannah's ignorance.

"Have I offended you?"

"No, ma'am. Just that we thought 'appen we would be famous an' all. Our families got a small pension from Mr Blackson. He was the owner, ma'am. An' I know that my mam kept a corner of the house for me. But I hoped that people would remember us. You's the first person we've been able to ask."

"You can tell me about it, John," Hannah offered.

"Not much to say, truth be told. If it 'adn't happened that day, it would have 'appened the next. Ten men started the climb to the surface, an' ten men never made it."

"You weren't a man then, Johnny," said the younger voice. "Just because you can speak nice an' all, don't make you a grown-up."

Hannah saw the dust particles swirl, as though John was turning around to admonish Pip, but he said nothing.

"You died here?" Hannah asked.

"No, ma'am. Like I said, in Saltilack, in Kernow. You call it Cornwall, I think."

"So why are you here now? You realise you're in London?"

"Yes, ma'am. Never thought as I'd get to London in my lifetime. Well...I didn't I s'pose. We didn't come here right away, you understand? For sixteen years we were in the shaft at Saltilack, warning the others, day and night. More days warning than not. That place was a grave, dressed as a tin mine. Alls we could do was knock though. Knock, knock. An' move things. Lunches. Pickaxes. Torches. One day, they closed the mine, and we thought we should leave for good. We just went. One moment in Saltilack. The next, somewhere where the language was different. Spent scores of years at a coal pit across the water, in Wales. Didn't matter that they spoke funny. We could still knock when there was danger, an' that was all the warning they needed. Even that place closed eventually, but the miners, they knew we were there and they told the owners not to close the shaft so we could get out and go to a new pit. They didn't realise that we didn't need a real exit.

"But I suppose there are no mines left, because we ended up here, under this abandoned lift shaft. It reminds us of ol' Saltilack. And here's where we knock, only the people, they're busy, and not miners. They don't know what the knocking means. They ignore it and pretend they can't hear it. But you didn't. You came."

"Why are you knocking now, John?"

"Because they will all die, ma'am. All of them. In a few days, they will all die."

Chapter 14

"WHO WILL DIE, JOHN?" Hannah asked. "And please call me Hannah."

"All of them, ma...Hannah."

"That's what you said. But who?"

The Knocker was silent, and Hannah thought he was avoiding the question, but she felt the air shift and realised he was moving back towards the door of the chamber. Patel must have sensed something too, because he recoiled and shivered as the disturbance passed him. Hannah nodded. "Yes, it's heading over there."

"I'm having a hell of a time working out what's going on from just your half of the conversation," he grumbled. "Someone's dying?"

The dust kicked up in a trail towards an alcove in the corridor. Hannah pointed at it, and Patel's eyes widened. "There's something there?"

"Yes, John Puddle. He's a...Knocker. An old miner, I think."

"I'm sixteen, Hannah," John said. "I didn't grow old. The mine took me before I got the chance."

"What's he doing here?" Patel asked.

"Keeping watch, I believe."

Knock, knock, knock.

The banging was loud and metallic.

"OK, I heard that!" Patel gasped. "Why can I hear it all of a sudden?"

John sounded patient. "You should tell your friend that it's because it will happen *here*. In Baker Street station. In this room. Everyone can hear the knocking in the place where's we's warning."

"He's suggesting it's because we are right on top of the problem."

"It's coming from the alcove," Patel said, pointing.

"That's where he is."

At first glance, the light from the strips wasn't going far into the recessed part of the wall, but then Hannah realised that's because the back of it was jet black, and not made from brick or tiles like the rest of the chamber. She put out a hand and touched cold metal, steel painted ebony. To her surprise, it moved a little under pressure.

"It's a baffle, Hannah," John said quietly. "Nothing but an old iron door. You should open it. I can't make myself whole enough to do it for you."

"What's a baffle?"

"Ventilation. A way of moving air around the mines. Well, I mean the underground railway station. I forgets sometimes that men don't search for ore here, just for time that they've already lost."

"You don't like the Tube, John?"

"I didn't enjoy being beneath the ground at all. What man would? But I never saw a railway like this when I was whole. I heard about them, mind, for taking rocks around the moor, but I never saw one with my own eyes, unless you count the cart in the shaft, but I don't like to remember that. These railways are demonic." He went quiet. "I s'pose we are the demons now."

"I don't think that's true," Hannah said. She gave the baffle a hard push, and it spun easily on bearings in the floor and ceiling. Patel jumped backward to avoid it, and Hannah caught it at the apex of its turn.

There was a sudden draft from the lift shaft behind them, drawn down into the tunnel beyond. The open baffle had revealed a platform. They were standing, looking through a grill high in the wall opposite; their feet level with the heads of the passengers staring vacantly towards them. Almost as soon as the baffle opened, and the wind whipped past them, it reversed and blew into the chamber. The reason became clear as an incoming train howled into the station, pushing a plug of air ahead of it that, with the ventilation open, had somewhere new to go.

Hannah stepped back involuntarily, but quickly realised she was completely safe. As the train sat humming in the station, she was fascinated to see it from an angle that normally would be inaccessible. A platform announcement echoed around the chamber, and then the shrill beeps of the closing doors. In less than thirty seconds, the electric motor whined into life, and the train exited, sucking air behind it once more. Hannah's coat billowed in the gale.

"Something is going to happen here?" she asked. "Next to the Jubilee Line platform?"

"Yes, Hannah. We know it will."

"And why are you warning us? Can we stop it?"

"That's never happened before," John said sadly. "We warned folk to get out before it did. But it always did."

"So, what am I supposed to do? Shut down the Tube network?"

The answer came not in words, but as a repeated banging on the baffle that echoed around the chamber. Hannah was sure she could see passengers on the platform looking straight at them, trying to trace the source of the noise.

"What's it saying?" Patel asked, covering his ears. Hannah waved at him to be quiet.

"John, you'll have to give us more than that. You normally warn miners of an impending disaster so they can save themselves. But here you say that everyone dies. So what's the point of warning anyone?"

"We always see death, Hannah. Whether that death happens or not is up to thems we warn."

"So, it's not set in stone. Can we prevent the death?"

The baffle banged again, as though the Knocker was reluctant to offer advice on how to avoid catastrophe.

"What is it?" Patel asked. "Like two knocks for yes, three for no?"

"Nothing that useful. Oh God. In the old days, I would have just checked in with Wayworthy. He would have known what to do."

"You still can," Patel reminded her. "Flynn has his memories."

"Yes, but not his wisdom. Not yet. It's as if he has to consult an encyclopaedia every time, and if the information isn't in there, filed under 'Knocker warnings', then he's not going to be able to join the dots with the stuff he *does* know."

"So, we'll do this the traditional way," Patel suggested. "I'll think of a way of flagging it to the powers that be. Although I'm not sure what I'm flagging. A ghost is telling a friend that some hurty things will happen?"

Hannah's eyes widened. "Of course! We don't actually know what's going to happen! John, is there an accident or something else? Terrorism maybe?"

"Whoa, hold on, Hannah." Patel grabbed her arm and pulled her aside. "What if the ghost is the one who's doing the deed?"

"He can't," she protested. "Moving this door is beyond him. How's he going to cause a disaster on the Tube?"

"You've only got his word for that."

"We've seen this before," John interrupted. The owners never wanted to listen to the men. We would knock for days, and the miners would be proper convinced that they would hit a gas pocket, or the ceiling would come down, and then they would tell the owners, but they never listened. We could have saved so many more. Don't let this owner ignore us like the rest."

"He's not an owner, John. He's a police officer. He can help."

"That may be so, ma'am." Hannah noticed that formality had returned. "But he is the one with the power. I can feel it. If you have sway over this man, then please use it to persuade him to do something."

"What would that help look like?"

Bang, bang, bang.

"Oh, this is useless," Hannah sighed. "Whenever I ask about specifics, we only get noise."

"Then I'll have to cover all the bases," Patel said, "but it's going to be tricky. I can flag an unspecified threat to the Jubilee line without anyone thinking it was unusual, but what if we are looking at an accident? Just a maintenance issue gone spectacularly wrong? I'll be laughed at."

"Let me try something else," Hannah suggested. She took a pause as another train screamed out of the station. "John, we want to listen. You want to be heard. But we can't help unless we know what we're dealing with. I don't understand why you can't just tell us, but I assume there is a reason. Maybe it's because you've never been able to talk before. Maybe it's that you don't know what to do with that power. You have to understand that this isn't like a mine in your day. There's not one shaft, a hundred miners, and a single owner. There are hundreds of miles of tunnels, millions of people, and a collection of owners that would make the bureaucracy you've seen before look like a playground squabble. If you truly want to find a way to stop whatever is going to happen from happening, you have to learn how to tell us more."

The chamber was quiet, with nothing more than a slight breeze from the ventilation shaft.

"Who the hell are you?" asked a coarse voice from the chamber. A man was standing at the entrance to the alcove, clad in hi-vis, and carrying a toolbox. He pointed a lit torch at them despite the lights being on, as though he had turned it on by habit.

"It's OK, pal," Patel said, "I'm BTP." He flashed his warrant card.

"OK, but who's she?" The man waved at Hannah. "And who the hell opened the baffle?"

"That was us," Patel admitted. "She's with me."

"You shouldn't be here," the man said, "polis or not. This is off-limits without the right authorisation. There's fragile kit in this room, and now it's blowing a hoolie. How did you get in?"

"Door was on the latch. Look, we were just investigating something. A tip off you might say."

"In which case it would have gone through the station controller, and he didn't tell me."

"So call it in," Patel suggested. "We'll sort this out."

The man rubbed a hand through his hair, then put it on the radio on his collar. He seemed to think better of it and rubbed his temples instead.

"Just get out of here, and next time, go through the right channels."

Patel looked at Hannah, who shrugged. "I don't think there is much more to be gained by standing here and talking to John."

"OK," Patel said. "We're all done anyway. I was getting cold in this draft.

"Aye," the man agreed. "It's a wee bit nippy down here at this time of year."

He watched Patel and Hannah cautiously as they filed out of the chamber and back into the brighter lights of the tunnel, then shut the door firmly behind them with a click.

Chapter 15

"YOU'VE NO IDEA HOW good it feels to have that knocking out of my head," Hannah said as they walked down Portland Place towards the clynic.

"It's gone completely?" Patel checked.

"I can't believe it was ever there. I hadn't realised that even when I couldn't actually hear it before, the rhythm was still in my brain, like a blood vessel pulsing. And now I feel as though I've woken up after a long migraine."

"I'm glad, but it's not all blue skies, is it?"

"I wanted to be normal...ish...for a while. I made myself park the issue with the headless lady, and even the cages, but this feels bigger. We can't stick our heads in the sand about a group of dead miners telling us there's an impending disaster on the Tube. This is human stuff."

Patel didn't answer.

"Can we?" Hannah checked.

"Police work is a lot about working out when to act and when to accept that most information is noise."

"You are saying this isn't real?"

"Oh, I believe the Knockers are real. But why should we trust them?"

They reached number fifty, and Hannah paused. "Because ignoring them might be costly. What do we lose by taking it seriously?"

"A lot of sleep and time, but sure. Not tonight, though. You said there were a few days, so we can pick it up tomorrow."

"Yeah, tomorrow." Hannah climbed the steps and realised that Patel remained standing at the bottom. "Are you coming in?"

"No," he said, grimacing. "I'm going to hit the sack. You should too."

"OK," Hannah said, with a tinge of disappointment. "Goodnight Shiv. I really did enjoy the first part of the evening."

"Yeah, me too." He blew her a kiss and walked north up the road, scratching the back of his head. Hannah watched him until the darkness won out and his figure disappeared into the gloom. She extracted the enormous key from her bag and let herself in, resting her back against the inside of the door for a moment before sliding down into a squat.

What the hell was that, Han? He couldn't have looked less interested in coming in if he tried.

She shook herself out of it.

You've always sucked at dating, so no need to be bothered by this one; that wasn't even a date anyway.

"How was the date?" Mia asked from the top of the stairs.

"Oh my God! You are like my mother," Hannah said. "But she never even let me get through the door before starting the interrogation, so I suppose this is a little better."

"Oh, not well, judging by your grump, darling."

"It was...unexpected," Hannah said.

Mia's mood shifted instantly. "Did he try something? Do I need to get...catty with him?" She raised her eyebrows.

"No, no. He was fine. It went awry after dinner—not his fault though."

"I'm sorry to hear that," Mia said. "Anything you want to talk about?"

Hannah started up the stairs. "Not tonight. I'm just about ready for sleep." Mia touched her shoulder as she passed, and Hannah acknowledged it with a smile. She threw her bag and coat onto her bed and slumped to the floor for the second time in a minute.

She marvelled at how much she needed a support network, but how fragile the one she had cobbled together now felt. Patel was tetchy, and there were motives there that she struggled to understand. Flynn was permanently overwhelmed. Mia, as friendly as she was on the surface, had an air of danger about her, and her father's presence still loomed large.

For a moment she wondered if Trundle might come through for her. After all, the troll's straight-talking could be just what was needed. But no, she didn't need blunt. She needed caring.

"Cup of tea," Hannah said to no one in particular and groaned herself off the floor and into the kitchen where the remains of the Flynn's dinner were still sitting in a pan on the hob. For such neat and tidy creatures by nature, they had a habit of leaving their meat-heavy leftovers all around the house, in a way that would have melted Wayworthy's brain.

She flicked on the kettle and wandered onto the landing, asking herself where Trundle, Ruadh, and Pascal were sleeping. The previous night, Flynn had insisted on the selkie and ogre crashing downstairs in the consulting room, but Trundle had received the privilege of a bed upstairs. It wasn't past midnight yet, so she was surprised the house was so quiet.

Behind her in the kitchen, she heard the kettle click off, but before she could head back and make a brew, she felt a draft on her face. The house was usually very warm, but this suggested a window was ajar. Maybe one of their guests preferred it on the cooler side or Flynn had left the roof open again.

Hannah, a wet finger in the air, followed the breeze into a storeroom at the rear of the house. She was aware that this was directly above the no-go zone area in the consulting room, and so the therianthropes avoided it like the plague. In fact, Flynn and Mia had taken to locking it in case the children went in by mistake. But the door wasn't locked now and, in fact, was swinging gently in the draft. It creaked softly.

She approached it cautiously, for reasons that she didn't understand. The closer she got, the stronger the breeze became, but also the louder the sound grew from within. Snoring.

Hannah pushed the door a couple of inches further open, enough to peer inside. The lights were off, but there was sufficient residual glow from the London streetlights to make out a shadow at the back of the room. An enormous grey figure was curled up on the floor. Its back moved up and down with a slow rhythm, its breathing steady and deep. It appeared to be sucking its thumb. Shelves had collapsed all around it, and it was nestled both on and among hundreds of books and files. It looked as though it had engaged in a struggle with the shelves and lost.

"Jeez, Pascal," she whispered. "What happened here?"

The ogre opened its eyes.

"Oh, sorry," she blurted, "I didn't mean to wake you."

It sniffed the air.

"Pascal?" Hannah said warily, unsure how much of the man was present in the beast. She forced herself to think of it as 'he' in case that made any difference.

"Hello," he rumbled, his accent a mishmash of French and something that defied description.

"You can't be comfortable there," she pointed out. "Why are you sleeping on the floor?"

The ogre thought for a moment, but Hannah wasn't sure if it was because he didn't know the answer, or he didn't know the right words.

"I am hot," he said eventually. "I feel wind from...here. I enter here to sit and be more cold."

"Oh, right, yes, I felt the breeze too." She looked at the window, which was firmly shut. "Although I don't know where it's coming from."

"I sit here, but then I change again. There is no space here, so I hit things. Sorry."

"You didn't realise that you were off the path in that corner? Of course not. I bet it was a surprise to you. I understand now why everything fell down. You are not small in that form."

Pascal looked at her blankly.

"I wish I spoke French," Hannah said sadly.

"I wish I not here," Pascal said, more sadly.

"Yes, I imagine you don't. And we'll see about that when we get a moment to breathe."

"Can I stay in this room? I do not want to be...like man."

Hannah smiled gently. Every LineFolk she had met spent their lives trying to appear human for fear of discovery. Even if they resented that disguise, they never suggested they preferred their true form. Pascal was endearingly honest.

"You can, of course. But I don't know how good it is for you to keep changing. Flynn says it's knackering."

"Knackering?"

"Tiring. Burns lots of energy. So you should try to stick to one form, and this corner, or downstairs in the consulting room, are the only places in London that I know it's safe to look like this. And you can't lie here forever. It might be best to change to human in the morning and stay that way until we can work out how to get you back home."

"Home."

"It really is very drafty in here," Hannah observed. "Maybe there is a gap in the floorboards."

She bent down and put a hand against the floor, but decided that the breeze was originating higher up. There were books strewn everywhere, and she picked her way through the debris of Pascal's transformation, to where one bookcase had been dislodged and was set at an angle to the wall. "This might have fallen on you," she said, realising that the air was coming from behind it. She gave the shelves a tentative push and was surprised that they moved easily, as though hinged. It pivoted shut, and the draft lessened, although it persisted, tangible through the small space between shelf and plaster.

"Does it work the other way?" she asked herself and pulled. The bookcase swung open until it hit a mound of literature on the floor that was too heavy to shift. There was now a foot-wide gap between the shelves and the wall. The breeze became a gust, and Hannah blinked as dust was dislodged from within and blew into her eyes. The smell of oil and dampness filled the room.

"Why am I surprised?" she asked Pascal, not expecting an answer. "This place is built out of secrets." The ogre leaned forward to see what she was looking at, then sensed the edge of the linepath and retreated quickly, pressing himself against the wall under the window.

"Hidden passageway," Hannah said, pointing into the darkness, marvelling at how calmly she was taking this revelation. "I hope there's nothing dodgy in there." She spent a moment thinking about what might be dubious enough for Wayworthy to have wanted to hide it behind a bookcase in a usually locked room.

"Light, I need light." Her phone was back by the kettle, so she flicked on the lights in the room. Pascal squinted and covered his eyes, assuming an expression of resignation that his sleep was going to remain disturbed for the foreseeable future. The paltry bulb, suspended without a shade from the ceiling, did little to improve visibility in the passageway. Hannah could see a yard into the gloom, just enough to observe more steps heading down. She tried to conjure a mental map of the premises. They were above the consulting room; that much was clear, but this wall was on the edge of the building, nestled against the adjoining property.

Did it go next door, or into a gap between the two buildings?

It was obvious that it was the latter, because the stairs doubled back on themselves in a small area, returning towards the house. Not wanting to enter without a torch, Hannah leaned into the void and saw that it was actually a spiral staircase as you might find in a castle turret, but with wooden treads that were surprisingly pristine, either through lack of use, or from regular maintenance.

"Am I going in?" she asked Pascal, who shrugged in reply.

"I'm going in," she said determinedly, "but with a torch."

Twenty seconds later, she had retrieved her phone. There was a message alert from Patel, and she swiped it aside, avoiding reading it. "Not now, Shiv," she muttered, then to Pascal. "Don't move until I'm back."

The steps were tight, and she hugged the outer edge, which was the only spot where the treads were wide enough to place a foot without it hanging over the lip. The bricks were rough, although there was a smooth trail at waist height as though a century's-worth of hands had been placed gently on the wall for support as people, or things, went up and down.

Hannah noticed that the breeze was intermittent. It was coming and going, and occasionally she felt it reverse direction, her hair whipping around her face as it was picked up from behind. She spat it out of her mouth, just one more thing to worry her as she descended. She quickly observed that she was heading below ground level with no sign of an exit into the clynic. Whoever constructed this passage was only interested in getting beneath the surface.

She tried to estimate how deep she was—maybe twenty metres—when she encountered a door, ajar like the bookcase entrance had been upstairs. Cautiously opening it, she found herself in a narrow corridor. She had long since lost her sense of direction, and the passageway might have been heading towards any point on the compass. Closing her eyes, she could feel linether flowing around her, so knew she was still on the linepath. She padded down the corridor, feeling crumbling concrete crunch under her shoes, but the linether remained. There was no sensation that it was moving with her, so she must be walking along, or deeper into, the safezone.

A dull rumble shook the tunnel, but no dust fell from the ceiling, suggesting that it was a frequent event. The shaking was accompanied by another gust of wind.

A train.

"Why does everything lead to the Underground in this city?" Hannah whispered. "And why did Wayworthy need access to the Tube tunnels? Wasn't it enough to be on top of them?"

"He liked to sit and watch the trains," a voice said in her ear.

Hannah screeched and dropped her phone, which clattered to the hard floor, the torch pointing down. For a second, while she scrambled to get it back, the tunnel was dark apart from a rectangle of light leaking from around the case onto the concrete.

"John Puddle, is that you?" she asked.

"Yes, ma'am. Sorry for scaring you again."

She felt her temples. So far, no sign of a returning headache, or any knocking for that matter.

"Why are you here and not at Baker Street?"

"I can be anywhere I want in the tunnels. I followed you along this one, the brown one. Then you stopped for a while. I thought I would have to start to knock."

"Please don't. I'm right here. Talk to me."

"The others didn't want me to do this. They told me we should stay all traditional and just knock. Let you work it out like everyone else has."

Hannah wasn't sure whether she felt flattered or insulted. "But you didn't believe I would?"

"No, ma'am, sorry. Not this time. What was it you said to me back at the baffle? If you truly want to find a way to stop whatever is going to happen from happening, you have to learn how to tell us more. I am learning, I think. It doesn't take much, just the will to do it. An' getting away from the others."

"OK, and you've found the will?"

A train passed noisily, but it didn't seem to affect her ability to hear John, who was somehow projecting his voice directly into her head.

"Yes, I don't have lots to tell you, but what I do is important."

"And that is?"

"Damps."

Chapter 16

Saltilack Tin Mine, Cornwall, England
1867 – fifteen years after the cart disaster

Click, clack. Click, clack.

The cart was heavy with ore, but thankfully not with men.

John Puddle watched it cautiously from a crosscut a few yards away. He knew the muckmen couldn't see him, but he was aware that, given the right circumstances, they could touch him, and he wanted to avoid any unnecessary bother for the miners. They would yell and swipe at the thin air. It made him feel unwanted and unloved. John hadn't enjoyed love in fifteen years, and he didn't need reminding.

The closest living man was Davie Farmer, Pip's younger brother, although now a strapping twenty-three-year-old and worth four men on his own. John had watched him as he descended nervously on his first shift, pausing with the other miners to cross their chests and doff their caps at the site of the abandoned seam where everyone had perished, before moving on to the deeper, newly exposed face. A hundred yards further, and a hundred yards of additional chain for the spindle on the surface to bear.

Davie whacked the links with the handle of his pick and, a thousand yards away, the spindle began to turn faster as the banksmen on the shafthead doubled their efforts at the signal. Jack marvelled at him and the man he had become. When he first came down, he was the same age as Pip had been, and alas would forever be, but as the years passed, Davie matured and now he looked more like he could have been Pip's uncle than his brother. It was hard to believe the order with which he and Pip had come from the same mother, as the younger ordered the other men around with calm assuredness, and the older scampered unseen among the miners, giggling and stealing their lunches.

Pip hadn't been like this when the accident happened. Like all the boys in the mine, he grew up fast underground, and he was already a little sullen. After the disaster things changed, and it was as though hitting the wall that day had stripped half a decade from him.

John picked at his fingernails, but the dirt never came out. It had sat there for fifteen years, along with the dust that coated every inch of skin. That wasn't the worst problem, though—it was boredom. At first, there had been confusion. Men and boys unpicked themselves from a tangle of metal and rock, marvelling at their survival after the terror of the fall, grinning at those who had been waiting at the bottom of the shaft, expecting the laughter of relief and promises of beer to be bought on the surface, but they were faced with shocked faces and sobs. The stares of the other men burned into them, but with horror they realised that the focus was behind them, in the wreckage. John turned slowly and saw his shattered body lying beneath a beam. He had been at the back of the cart and had taken the full force of the impact. His arms were in the wrong place, and his legs seemed to be missing altogether.

"What's up wi' us?" Pip had wailed. He was swiping his hand repeatedly through one of the upright beams as though it were made of water.

John had watched as the boy tried to climb up the shaft, but something held him back, and his feet slid on the spot like a dog on an ice-covered lake.

It wasn't the last time the group attempted to leave the mine, but every attempt resulted in failure. Most of them came to terms with being dead before too long, although the shock of not being in heaven took longer. What didn't come easily was the realisation that they would be here forever. "Ol' Saltilack will be here for a thousand years," Michael had said, and there was little reason to argue with him. People would always need tin, right? But that didn't make it easy. John longed to see his family again. The married men were equally desperate, and many were tormented by the thought that their wives would have forgotten them and found new loves.

"We's Knockers," Elias had sadly informed them all one day, or was it night? It was meaningless now—the passage of time marked only by the changing of the shifts. "The first to die in this hell, so there wasn't none to warn us before. Now it's our job to warn others."

"Wa's a Knocker Pap?" Pip had asked as he tried to steal an apple from a passing miner—fruit that he could never actually eat.

"A miner's spirit, boy. One with a solemn duty to protect our brothers."

"I don't like solemn," Pip laughed.

"Well, like it or not, lad, you'll be doing it."

"But how?" John had asked. "I can't smell none. I can't taste neither. I can barely touch, but only if I think as hard as I ever did in my life." He paused. The mention of life felt like a blade in the hearts of many of the men.

"You can see and hear, can't you?" Elias had insisted. "And there is nothing better to do here, so you will pay attention to things, even when the men working are too tired to lift a pick."

The Knockers had grudgingly agreed, and for years they took turns in the gaps between shifts to search carefully for evidence of damaged supports or listen for straining seams. Occasionally they would spot something and rap hard on the nearest piece of wood until the miners paid attention and fixed the problem. After a while, the living began to appreciate the dead, doffing a cap to them at the start of the day and leaving morsels of food as offerings. John appreciated that more than anything because he knew that food was scarce. He often licked his lips, remembering the bread he was excitedly planning to buy on the evening he died.

It was a morning like any other when he realised that he had a gift that the other Knockers didn't share.

John didn't sleep now that he was dead, but he did have periods when he tried to switch off from the watching and the listening, letting some of the others take on the responsibility. But he found that those moments allowed his mind to stray, not into places of his imagination, but into the future, and the clarity he was developing. For John no longer needed his eyes and his ears to see danger. He could feel it coming like a barrel rolling down a hill. Not limitless foresight, but good enough to make a difference. At first, the others didn't believe him. He told them about a crack that would appear in the seam, so tiny as to be missed by everyone, but resulting in a catastrophic collapse in a couple of days' time. It would just take one mighty heave from the new boy, Davie, Pip's brother. The boy said, in a haughty tone, that was nonsense, because Davie wasn't even in the mine yet, but lo-and-behold, the very next shift, Davie descended, looking as green as the grass on the hill behind the pithead. You've never seen a group start knocking so quickly. They knocked furiously for a day and a night until the miners refused shifts because of the fear of what was going to happen. The manager came down himself, a rare treat for all, and looked around the seam. It was only a minute's inspection that revealed the fissure, and he ordered immediate bolstering of the tunnel.

From that moment onwards, the Knockers always listened to John, and the miners always listened to the Knockers.

Now John watched Davie, feeling proud that he had grown into the fine man that John himself had planned to be, but never would. The young miner dropped to his haunches, taking a second to rest while the cart was making its ascent. While Davie took a moment, John also switched off.

That opened his mind.

And for the first time in fifteen years, he could smell.

It was eggy, and after more than a decade, it was overwhelming.

John stared at Davie. How could he not smell this? It was worse than the time his sister had left the duck eggs in the sun for the afternoon, then cracked them into a bowl, filling the house with the most rotten stink imaginable. Maybe one man had brought something unspeakable down into the mine and discarded it to rot in a corner. Reluctantly, he decided that he wasn't smelling a thing that was already here; rather, he was picking up something that *would* be here.

But it was just a bad smell.

He headed back down the crosscut where the other Knockers were lounging around, apart from the perennially active Pip.

"Elias, Michael," he called out to the older men. "Can I speak wi' you?"

They were always glad of a distraction to break the years of boredom.

"I had a vision," John began. "Only not seeing as such. This time I can smell something."

They laughed. "We hasn't smelled anything for fifteen years, John," Elias pointlessly reminded him

"I know," he frowned. "Tha's why I think it's important."

"What are you sniffing, John?" Elias continued. "Michael's armpits?" He wasn't taking this seriously.

"Not any of you! Something as rotten as his pits, though."

"What's that, John?" Michael asked, leaning in.

"Eggs. Bad ones. I can smell it now."

"Can ye now? Has you smelled anything else recently?"

"No, this is the first thing in...well...a long time."

"An' you are sure that the men can't smell it too?"

"Young Davie can't, and I was sitting right by him when it first appeared. It's so strong, Michael. It must be one of my visions."

"I hear that," Michael said slowly, then looked at the rest of the group. "Right lads, we's got some knocking to do."

"What? Why?" John asked. "What is it, Michael?"

"Stinkdamp, my boy. Sewer gas. Sulfurated hydrogen."

John tried to repeat that quietly, but his tongue tangled up in the syllables. He'd never heard such a long word in his life. "Is that bad?"

"It'll knock out a cow and kill her stone dead. I hate to think what it would do to Davie and the boys. I smelled it once up at Tresko, a league deep. The foreman had us out of that mine before I could even grab my pick. It's a quiet killer, lad, and get enough of it and it will go with a bang an' all. My guess is that they are going to hit a seam of fool's gold soon. It goes hand in hand with the stinkdamp."

"Right, lads," Elias shouted. "Knock for all you're worth!"

To a man and a boy, they started banging on beams, tools, and even the rock face itself. A cacophony of knocks filled the crosscut and echoed down into the main chamber.

Out of the corner of his eye, John saw Davie leap to his feet, and within a few seconds he was joined by the other miners on the shift. They began to inspect the shaft, the seam, and anything that could be dangerous if less than perfect.

"It's not that!" John shouted, but of course Davie nor any of the men could hear him. "You won't smell it yet, and by the time you do, it might be too late."

For a second, it appeared that Davie paused and listened to the stagnant air from the shaft; then he shrugged and began his visual inspection again.

"Davie, listen to me," John screamed, almost right into the miner's ear, but to no avail.

Twenty minutes later, the experienced men pronounced the seam all clear, and despite the frantic knocking extending deep into the night, and a few nervous glances towards the surface, the toil of extracting the ore continued uninterrupted.

***

An extract from 'A History of Cornish Tin Mines'. The closure of Saltilack

As tin mines go, Saltilack was young when its end came. Bringing ore up from beneath the seabed was an engineering marvel, and so it opened later than many, but closed after only thirty-five years, following the tragic death of twenty-six men in an 1867 accident. Coming only fifteen years after a cart disaster killed ten, the mine was declared unsafe—an unusual practice at the time—and attention shifted to more profitable and reliable seams inland.

Mechanical failure was blamed for the first incident, but no blame was apportioned for the second. A method to detect a build-up of poisonous Hydrogen Sulphide gas had not yet been invented, and even to this day, it is normally only found in trace amounts in mines. On April 10th, 1867, the third shift was waiting at the pithead for the outgoing miners to emerge, but the signal to lift the cart never came. Two volunteers descended the diagonal shaft using rudimentary climbing equipment and discovered the entire shift unmoving, and mostly dead, at the bottom. The acrid smell of rotten eggs immediately told them the cause, and they quickly exited, bringing the bad news to the surface.

A vigil was mounted at the entrance, hoping that some of the miners might have recovered and surfaced, but none did. The possibility of death was considered too great for any other men to risk their lives retrieving the bodies, and the shaft was sealed seven days later.

That event was mired in controversy as the workers bricking up the entrance heard a frantic banging from within, which they attributed to the Knockers—benevolent spirits that protect miners—but some of the families thought may actually be survivors. The sealing of the shaft continued, and a small opening was left for two further days to allow the Knockers to leave if they wished. Eventually, even that was closed up, and Saltilack Mine was consigned to history.

Chapter 17

HANNAH RACED BACK UP the stairs, her shoes scuffing on the rough brickwork steps. Pascal still huddled in the no-go corner as she entered the main building, but she gave him barely a glance as she ran onto the landing.

"Flynn! Mia!" she shouted, but it wasn't just the werecats who emerged; Ruadh and Trundle joined them, coming to see what was causing the midnight commotion.

"Drawing room, now," Hannah ordered, unbothered if the troll and the selkie also got to hear what she had discovered.

"First thing," she said to the cats, "did you know there is a secret staircase down to the Bakerloo Line under this building?"

"Secret what?" Flynn asked.

"Tunnel, staircase. From the storeroom at the back of this floor."

"That's usually locked."

"Yep, until Pascal was hunting for somewhere cooler to sleep and snapped the lock, then broke half the fixtures because he didn't realise it was a no-go zone in there and unexpectedly went all ogre on us. There are stairs behind a bookcase."

"Nonsen..." Flynn started, then saw Hannah's expression and just said, "OK."

"Did you go *down*?" Mia asked, her eyes shining brightly as they always did when there was a hint of intrigue and danger.

"Of course I did, wouldn't you? And I met an old friend down there. A Knocker, called John Puddle."

"Darling, you don't have friends," Mia reminded her. "And what's a Knocker?"

"A dead miner," Hannah replied, inwardly marvelling at the fact that this statement was accepted without question by her present company. "He can see the future. As long as it's mine-related, or tunnels, or something. Look, I'm not sure what the parameters are, but the important thing is that he is predicting a disaster on the Tube within a couple of days."

"You shouldn't listen to phantasms," Flynn said. "Remember, they are echoes of their former human selves. Doomed to repetition."

"I've only met two of them, and they both seemed to be in full control. John's got history. He and his fellow Knockers warned miners for a century before they moved to the underground railways, but usually it's tunnel collapse. This is not the same. He says it's gas."

"I know that phantasms are distinct from LineFolk, and that both can do incredible things, but I've never come across any with the gift of foresight. It seems unlikely."

"Do you want to take the risk?"

"I have a different question," Flynn said. "Why should we care?"

Hannah gawped at him.

"Yes," he said nervously and less convincingly, "why should the LineFolk care? Accidents happen to dwellers all the time."

"A poisonous gas on the Tube, and you don't think that you have an interest in that?"

"It will likely be a dweller act, aimed at harming other dwellers. I must draw a line somewhere."

"Will it?" Hannah snapped.

"The odds suggest that yes. Millions of dwellers in the city, but only a fraction of that number of LineFolk. And those who do inhabit the Tube tunnels, well, they are...not like the rest of us LineFolk. There is no helping them. Plus, human history tells us that dwellers are not averse to horrible acts of mass violence against each other."

"And recent experience tells me that LineFolk also have a taste for that," Hannah retaliated.

"You know something else, don't you, darling?" Mia said. "You're not guessing."

"John had his first vision a few days ago, right when I started hearing the tapping sound. He traced what he saw to Baker Street station—to a ventilation chamber off the Jubilee Line. A man deploying something in the tunnel. He and the others watched and waited in that chamber, and last night he came."

"The man?"

"Men actually, but yes, looking at locations, testing airflow."

"But they were still dwellers."

"Wrong. One of them wasn't, for sure."

"How do you know? More importantly, how does your deceased miner friend know?"

"Because one of them had a tattoo. John described it precisely. A snake eating its own tail, wrapped around his neck."

"Oh," Flynn gulped, glancing at Mia.

"Exactly," Hannah said triumphantly, pleased to have outflanked the werecat's skepticism, however petty that was.

"Why in the eternal serpent would *he* want to harm dwellers or LineFolk? Like all of us, his focus is on hiding effectively in the world that we are forced to share with them."

"I don't know," Hannah admitted, "but he's not cut from the same cloth as you are, or Wayworthy for that matter, despite their being related." She scratched her head. "I'm going to Shiv with this. I think this is a job for the police now."

"Who is Shiv?" Flynn and Mia asked in unison, then smiled at each other and said, "Jinx."

"That was very cute," Hannah admitted, "but I wish you'd done it when I was in the mindset to actually enjoy it. Shiv is Patel. It's his given name."

"No!" Flynn said. "And no debate, please. You can't bring the dweller police into this, not if Grubb is involved."

"Can you hear yourself?" Hannah asked, exasperated. "Patel isn't allowed to help when it's a LineFolk thing, and now he can't help when the concern is LineFolk killing humans. When *is* he allowed?"

"It's complicated, Hannah," Mia suggested. "Yes, Patel is an asset to us sometimes, but he's still a dweller. Can you imagine what would happen if this went beyond him, to others in the police? That might be it for the LineFolk. The endgame."

"It's going to be the endgame for an awful lot of Londoners if Grubb is allowed to do what he's planning."

"What *is* he planning, Hannah?" Flynn asked. "Did your pet phantasm tell you that, or was it just 'gas'?"

"John doesn't know for sure, but he's driven to stop it."

"Why? He doesn't breathe, I imagine."

"Because that's why he and the Knockers exist. To help those in trouble under the ground. Nearly two hundred years ago, he watched helplessly as twenty-five men died from gas poisoning because he wasn't able to talk and tell them exactly what would happen. There were boys he had seen grow up in the mine, and then he watched them suffocate. Now he knows it's going to happen again."

"He's not so helpless any more, then? Found his tongue?"

"You can be such a wanker sometimes," Hannah snapped. "Knockers only knock. It's in the name. Until he met me."

"Your ability to chat with previously silent phantasms is becoming ridiculous," Flynn sulked. "Alright. Assuming all of this is actually happening, and with going to Patel being out of the question, what do you propose we do?"

"Is that an admission that someone has to do something?"

Flynn shrugged, still smarting from Hannah's insult.

"I'll have to return to Grubb's," Hannah insisted. No one said anything. "No, lovely Hannah," she said sarcastically. "Don't put yourself at risk by going back to the evil abclynician's lair. Anyone?"

"Darling," Mia purred. "We aren't stopping you because we *know* Grubb. He's one of us. The only thing that he has done to truly hurt us is steal Axton's patients."

"Fine, but I'm still going. I'll find out what's what, and then you'll all see."

"I'll go with you," Ruadh said. "Before I was left for dead there, I went several times as a patient, although he told me I was more human than he would like me to be."

Hannah, Flynn, and Mia turned to the selkie.

"I mean it," she insisted. "I'll come with you. My father works on the lines, and who knows if he'll be impacted by the gas like a dweller would be. I want to help, to keep him safe."

"You haven't recovered yet," Flynn said, pointing at her arm, still in a sling against her chest. The selkie gave it an experimental wiggle and winced at the pain.

"There's no chance you would get down the ladder at Grubb's," Hannah said. "But thanks, I appreciate the support. It's in short supply tonight." She raised her eyebrows at the werecats.

"We should go in the back entrance," Ruadh said matter-of-factly.

"You can do that?" Hannah asked. "He told me it was a one-way system."

"He can't stop us from walking in the opposite direction. We just have to find the exit. I must have used it ten times over the years. I think I remember where it is."

"You are doing this right now?" Mia asked. "At two in the morning?"

"It will be quiet," Hannah said.

"And Grubb will definitely be there," Flynn pointed out.

"He sleeps in that dungeon!?" Hannah exclaimed.

"All abclynicans live on the premises."

"I get that when the option is a ten million pound property in central London, but he works out of an old air-raid shelter."

"I told you, dedicated to the cause."

Hannah was beginning to believe Flynn might be a secret Grubb fanboy.

"We'll see. Come on Ruadh. Coat on. We are going hunting for clues."

Chapter 18

HANNAH WAS DELIGHTED, AS were her tired feet, when Ruadh reminded her that selkies had no problem riding in a taxi. "I can't change without my pelt, so I can go anywhere I want in this godforsaken city."

"You are the first LineFolk that I've heard say 'God' and not 'the Serpent'."

"Their serpent does nothing for me. Mind you, neither does your god. I'll look after myself, thank you."

They got out at Notting Hill Gate station, and Hannah led Ruadh north up Pembridge Road until they reached a parade of shops and cafes. The streets were quiet, and their only company was a lone fox, who stopped and watched them cautiously before trotting without a care in the world towards some rubbish sacks awaiting collection.

"It's here somewhere," Hannah said. "I left in a hurry, so I didn't pay attention to exactly where. Between two shops, I remember that much."

Ruadh took a couple of strides into the street and looked around intently. "The smell of coffee is pretty strong as you open the door out of the tunnel, so I'm guessing it's near there." She pointed at a coffee shop a few metres away.

"That rings no bells," Hannah admitted, "but I did trip up a step on the way out. Might have just been my clumsy feet though."

"There," Ruadh nodded at a recessed doorway between the coffee shop and a clothes store next to it. "Look at the step up. Big enough to fall over?"

"If you're me, for sure."

They approached the alcove. The door was set back at least two metres, and the light from the street didn't penetrate that far. The floor of the passage was lined with black and white tiles in a checkerboard pattern. Hannah could see that footprints had been worn into the surface, like dinosaur tracks on a Dorset beach. One, two, three steps and out. How many beings had taken this route over the years, on their way from the clynic?

There was no handle visible on the door. In fact, there was no hardware at all apart from a keyhole, making it impossible to tell on which side it hinged, or whether it opened in or out. Hannah gave it a tentative push, but nothing happened. She hooked her fingernails under one of the panel edges and pulled, but only succeeded in splitting a nail. She sucked her finger while she considered the next steps.

"Are we surprised it's locked?" Ruadh asked. "I'm not."

"It was worth a try. Maybe we do need to go in the front entrance."

"Are we sneaking or knocking?"

The question was so stupid that Hannah didn't give it the time of day at first, then she realised she didn't know the answer. "I imagined sneaking, but come to think of it, why don't we just knock?"

"Because it's the middle of the night, plus you don't want to ask him whether he's planning a terrorist attack on the London Underground. What's he going to say to that? Good catch, ladies. Let me murder you where you stand to keep you quiet."

"But the door is locked," Hannah whined, immediately aware of how pathetic this made her sound.

Ruadh looked up at the ceiling, for all the world as though she was expecting divine intervention from a god that she didn't believe in, but it seemed it was merely exasperation. "Don't they teach humans anything useful at school? I didn't even go to one, but I know how to pick a lock."

"You do?"

"Uh, huh."

"Do you make a habit of breaking into places?"

"You really aren't LineFolk are you?" Ruadh said with a slight scowl. "I forget humans just have it all handed to them on a plate."

"Well, do you make a habit of it?"

"It's useful. I don't like to, and with my father working, I haven't had to for a while, but I bet I still have it." She reached for her mess of hair and pulled out a couple of pins, which hadn't seemed to do very much. "Do you have a bank card?"

"No, I left all my stuff back at the clynic. I was planning to break and enter. I wasn't going to carry ID with me."

"I thought dwellers lugged that kind of crap around with them everywhere."

"Wait!" Hannah patted her pockets. "I have this?" She held out a scrappy piece of card.

Ruadh peered at it. "A chicken shop loyalty card?"

"Yeah, don't judge me. But can you use it?"

The selkie twiddled it between thumb and forefinger. "Maybe. It feels a little like it's been through the wash, but I'm used to dealing with things that have been in water."

Hannah realised this was the same coat she had been wearing for her interview at the clynic, the day when the heavens had opened, and she had presented herself to Wayworthy as a drowned rat. The loyalty card was like a time capsule from a previous life. She had barely eaten fast food since then.

"Can you work with it?" she asked, not entirely sure what Ruadh was planning.

The selkie grimaced. "I'll try." She immediately squatted in front of the door and put an ear to the wood, tapping it gently in various places. "Hmm," she muttered, "I assumed there would be a complex internal mechanism, but I think it's just a regular, single-bolt lock."

"Why would he rely on that?" Hannah asked. "It doesn't seem very secure."

"Maybe he doesn't feel the need to be secure," Ruadh guessed. "Or more likely, there are more things inside to deter trespassers than a bit of sliding metal." This didn't appear to put her off. She stuck the pins into the keyhole at different angles, then slid the card into the gap between the door and the frame. Hannah tried to see what was happening, but Ruadh's movements were simple and fast. She stood up suddenly.

"Oh, you failed," Hannah said sadly.

"No, I didn't," Ruadh protested and pushed the door gently. It creaked open. She retrieved her hairpins and shoved them somewhere back into her red mane.

"Oh God," Hannah sighed. "I didn't think you'd actually manage it. I'm not prepared for what comes next." She had always been a law-abiding citizen, and despite everything that had happened in the last few months, this felt dangerously illegal. Skirting the fringes of what the LineFolk considered normal was one thing. Breaking human laws was real.

"This is your idea," Ruadh reminded her. "I'm just here for back-up."

Hannah took a tentative step over the threshold, reminding herself why they were here. John had seen Grubb preparing something in the chamber at Baker Street station, a place where the abclynician had no good reason to be, and where the Knocker had had a premonition of impending disaster.

The passageway was dark, so she turned on her phone torch, casting it around to get a sense of their surroundings. On her journey out a few days previously, bare lightbulbs had lit the way, but they were now off with no obvious switches. Like Grubb's chambers themselves, the walls were lined with old posters, some peeling, but some of which appeared to have become part of the plaster itself—flashes of the past burned into permanence by the passing of time.

Their shoes crunched on grit and pebbles. In the quiet of the night, they were like gunshots. Hannah slipped out of hers and nodded at Ruadh to do the same. Better to risk sore toes than to wake Grubb.

After fifty metres, where there were no doors off the passage, they reached a T-junction. Hannah had no recollection of which way she had come, but Ruadh pointed to the right, and they crept in that direction. Hannah could feel the linether flowing around them as they neared the Underground tunnels. Grubb's clynic was nearby.

Another bend in the passageway and the beam of the torch illuminated something familiar—the reception desk. Grubb's consulting room was just to their left, and the door was open.

Feeling like a special forces soldier, Hannah raised a fist in the air and Ruadh stopped on the spot. The silence was overwhelming. Not even the trains whispered from the tracks at this time of night. "Where do you think he sleeps?" she asked as quietly as she could manage.

The selkie shrugged, but adopted a thoughtful look and said, "Probably not in his office. I've never seen a bed there."

Hannah nodded and led the way into the consulting room. She waved the torch around, and it picked up the desk, chairs, and an array of filing cabinets.

"Oh, this is impossible," she muttered and looked for a light switch.

"Really?" Ruadh asked, realising what she was thinking.

"He's not here, so if we keep the door closed, what harm can it do?"

When the bulb illuminated, the contrast was shocking, and they squinted at each other for a good twenty seconds before it became bearable again. Hannah noticed that it was far brighter than on her previous visit, when the room's dim desk lamps had cast shadows. Grubb preferred it dark when he was there.

"We shouldn't have done this," Ruadh said out of the blue.

"Too late for that," Hannah retorted, her irritation obvious. "Let's poke about and see what we can find."

"He won't have left anything incriminating lying around."

"Don't be so sure," Hannah said. "My short experience with Line-Folk tells me that they are very casual with information security." She started opening drawers, looking for something out of the ordinary; however, an abclynic was never conventional, and they were full of junk of various types. This was nothing like Flynn's practice. She had been surprised at how disorganised that was, but had to admit that there was a system, and it worked. Grubb seemed to operate on a wing and a prayer, and his filing was in keeping with this.

"Have you looked under T for terrorism?" Ruadh suggested, but Hannah ignored her. She was grateful that the selkie had got her this far, but found it hard to understand her motivation. She was helpful one minute, sarcastic and obstructive the next. The selkie wasn't assisting right now, sitting on Grubb's desk in a way that made Hannah nervous, and experimenting with different positions for her sling.

It was halfway through the wall of cabinets that she found something interesting. Several of the drawers had contained machinery, but it was all covered in a layer of dust that suggested it hadn't been touched in a long time. This one housed pipework, wrapped into a vague cube shape, that was clean and polished. It was recently in use.

"Hello," Hannah said and reached in to pull it out. It was heavy, suggesting a dense metal was at work, but flexed slightly in her grip, as though it was loosely, or poorly, assembled. She placed it on Grubb's desk before it fell apart. It looked like a school science project.

"What's that?" Ruadh asked.

"I don't know, but it's only recently been put in that drawer. No dust." Hannah paced around the contraption, squatting slightly to bring it to eye-level. "I wish Flynn were here," she murmured. "He would know what this is. It's not electric—there's no plug or batteries. And what's this?" She pointed at a bottle, upside down with its neck in a rubber receptacle. She poked it, and it flexed. Cheap, thin plastic, like a used cola bottle.

"I wouldn't fiddle with that too much," a voice said from above. "Not unless you want an unfortunate end to your sojourn through my chambers tonight. It's a prototype only, but still reasonably lethal in clumsy hands."

Ruadh gasped and fell from the table, crying out in pain as she jarred her broken arm. Hannah snatched her fingers away from the bottle and looked up. She cursed herself for not checking the high ceiling of the room.

Grubb was suspended upside down from the beams across the roof. His neck was bent at an unusual and impossible angle, so his face was parallel to the floor. He had wrapped his arms protectively around his chest and swayed imperceptibly as though he had been perfectly still until the act of speaking had made him shift in the air.

"I should have known. You and Wayworthy are just the same," Hannah muttered. "He once said that he could sense me a mile off. You knew we were here before we even opened the door."

"My brother was better at that kind of thing than me," the mage replied, "but I have good hearing, and you are not stealthy." He looked at Ruadh. "What have you brought her here for? I thought I told you I wanted nothing to do with his ridiculous selkie slavery."

"Still clinging to the belief that gives you a conscience?" Hannah sneered. Her neck was aching from looking up into the rafters.

"Everything seems black and white to you, Miss Chadwick," Grubb calmly replied. He slowly unhooked a bare foot from the beam around which it curled—Hannah was sure for a moment that it was abnormally elongated, but that passed almost immediately—then bent upwards from his waist to grab that beam with a hand, before pivoting like a gymnast until he was hanging from a single arm. He gestured with a toe at the machine on the table. "Would you mind? I imagine I can survive a two-metre drop to the floor, but I'd rather tread onto my desk as I normally do."

Hannah found herself complying, unsure why, and Grubb let go, alighting cat-like onto the table with a small grunt.

"Your ability to perceive me only through stark extremes is ironic," he purred. "You cling so tightly to that fence you sit on that I would have thought you understood the concept of nuance in our world."

"Fence?"

Grubb adopted a mocking falsetto. "Am I human? Am I LineFolk? Oh, I don't know; I'll try being both." He dropped back to his normal voice. "Ladies, sit," he said and gestured for them to find a chair. "My man is not here at the moment, so you'll have to excuse my lack of hospitality." He put on a whiny tone again. "Oh, and it's four in the morning, so why should I care?"

"Do you know why we're here?" Hannah asked.

"I believe you were debating whether to ask me if I was planning an act of terrorism. Assuming that you would decide that to be rather rude, I would imagine your alternative option was to break and enter, then look for evidence that I was intending such an act."

"Are you?"

"Ah, back to option one. I admire that. Settle down, and I will, as they say, spill the beans. I'm confident that by the end you'll have come round to my point of view, and even if you don't...no matter." Grubb settled into a chair with a creak of straining fibreglass. "Let me ask you both some questions," he said. "Would you consider it important that the LineFolk continue to maintain their disguise?"

"Of course," Hannah replied. "I don't think the world is ready for a grand reveal."

"Do you accept that the nature of the Ouroborus means that LineFolk must likely continue hiding in London?"

"I don't know enough about the other options to answer that."

"There are no other options," Grubb said curtly.

"Then yes."

Why are you letting him drive the conversation?

"Would it therefore be risky if anything were to threaten the viability of that option? Peculiar consequences of other activities, you might say."

Hannah thought of the unintended side-effects of Tarrin's plan to transmit linether across the city and drain the Ouroborus to a dangerous level. "Yes. What are you telling us?"

"The Serpent's power is not eternal, ladies. Of course, we refer to it as though it were. No one is gatekeeping its use. But trust me, it is finite, and that end is coming sooner than I am comfortable with."

"Wayworthy never mentioned this. He thought it was fine to tap into the swerves and release even more of the linether."

"Well, of course he did. That was his solution, but it was shortsighted and unambitious. How much longer would that have powered the Ouroborus? A few months, perhaps? The plague pits are old, and those batteries are not what they once were. To truly bring it back to its peak, we need fresh blood. Literally."

Hannah caught his glance at the contraption on the desk.

"What is that?" she asked.

"Think of it as a way of unlocking enough power to keep the Ouroborus flowing for a century—a fusion generator for the linether, if you will."

"This thing makes linether?" Ruadh asked, putting a finger on the pipes.

"Please," Grubb interjected. "Do not touch it. You have no idea what you are playing with."

"Tell us then," Hannah suggested, moving a hand towards the contraption as provocation.

"Yes, it's possible, but no, this does not create it directly. All this does is encourage the conditions for the linether to recharge. You know, death and destruction, in this case through the medium of a little elemental gas I cooked up. Not linether, but a physical symbiotic miasma that uses it as its conduit. Rather deadly. It taps into a deep-seated part of the human brain, ironically the one that creates distrust and hatred, then activates it to an unmanageable level. Any dweller who comes into contact with this will literally hate themselves to death." He chuckled. "Elegant, don't you think?"

Hannah let her jaw drop as she struggled to find the words. "This is targeted at humans only. You are going to release this...miasma somewhere and mass-murder people. Does it kill LineFolk in human disguise as well? Would it kill me? You can't do this."

"This has been lovely," Grubb said, ignoring the question, "but I am sensing that you are having difficulty adjusting to the reality of the situation. Both situations. The one in this room, and out there, on the lines."

"Why were you at Baker Street station?" she asked as Grubb moved towards them. "Is that where it's happening?"

"It's obvious that you are clinging a little too tightly to the human identity that you still crave. So it's time for us to draw a line under the conversation, and for you to enjoy some reflection," he said in response.

"Who was the man you were creeping around with?"

Grubb's eyes flicked to Ruadh. "Into the strongroom, dweller."

"I'm not a dweller," the selkie replied calmly.

"I know you're not, which is why I was speaking to her, and you, as always, are just the incentive." In a flash, Grubb snatched Ruadh's wrist and yanked her off the desk and into his arms. She wriggled, but he put pressure on her broken arm, and she stopped with a sharp intake of breath, her back pressing against his chest.

"Let her go," Hannah commanded, momentarily forgetting the contraption. She had faced worse than Grubb in the last few weeks and had no fear about breaking his grip on the selkie.

She was foolish to be so confident.

Grubb grinned, a wide, sneering smile that opened across his face like an earthquake fault line. The corners were...wrong, spreading towards his ears as his mouth became more of a gash.

Where had she seen a jaw like this before? As a snakelike tongue whipped in and out between sharp-looking teeth, she remembered.

"You're a haemovore," she gasped. "How are you changing here in the safezone?"

"I know you've met the Countess," Grubb hissed. "After all, she helped to destroy my handiwork in Golden Square."

Golden Square. The transmitter! Of course, Grubb was involved!

"You'll know that we have some control of our form within the embrace of the linether. I'm not going to grow my wings here, but I can certainly bite." He opened his mouth wide and leaned in towards Ruadh's neck.

"Stop!" Hannah screamed. Grubb paused, his tongue licking the selkie's jaw in a sickening fashion. He looked at Hannah, inviting her to make the next move. She reached out with her mind, trying with all her might to sense his bones, muscles, and other tissue—determined to reverse his transformation as she had done with Tarrin, and give Ruadh the confidence to fight free,

He cocked his head at the sensation and sneered. "Oh, please. That might work on your common or garden werecat, but my kind is significantly more ancient and adept." Hannah felt a mental shield drop around him and her link to his abnatomy was severed abruptly.

"How can you be Wayworthy's brother?" she asked. "He was nothing like you."

"I told you," Grubb replied smugly. "We once were brothers in body, but that was a very, very long time ago. In the end, we were brothers only in mind. My own master was a mage like him, but he chose me, a haemovore, as his apprentice. Julius was already Julius by that point. He never liked it, but he tolerated it, even biting his tongue enough for us to continue to share a clynic, and to collaborate on writings. For a while, at least."

"You don't look a day over thirty."

"Why, thank you, my dear. Dweller blood can do that for a man. Well, not strictly speaking a man."

Ruadh struggled again as he ran a hand over her arm. "Selkie blood is salty. I don't really like it, but it's nutritious."

"You eat humans?"

"Why not? They are meaningless in our world. Just a pestilence on the lines that we could do without." He paused, and the smile returned. "Well, not completely. We do need them for the linether."

"LineFolk death powers the phantasms. Dweller death powers the serpent." Hannah let her voice trail off as she joined the dots.

A look of genuine admiration crossed Grubb's hideously split face. "Maybe you are what they whisper you are?" he mused. "But yes, of course. Dweller deaths by the hundreds of thousands created the plague pits and set the Ouroborus up for centuries. Now, a new wave of death will do it again."

Chapter 19

"YOU ARE GOING TO kill hundreds of thousands?" Hannah repeated, her jaw hanging in disbelief.

"No, of course not. Just a few hundred will do for now." Grubb was simultaneously sneering at her stupidity while assuming her acceptance of the situation.

"You're a lunatic."

"Ah, that is the old Hannah Chadwick talking. The new Hannah, the one I assume my brother intended to convert you into once you embraced your newfound abilities, surely understands that dwellers and LineFolk have been dancing around each other for centuries. They take a few of us, for sport, out of spite, because we are different. We take a few of them—for food, for fun, for the betterment of the serpent. I merely propose that, for a day, we shift that balance and recharge the Ouroborus for a decade."

"They won't let it happen. They'll fight back. Get revenge."

"They won't know who did it," Grubb scoffed. "I'm not sending a pack of weevils marauding through Baker Street station. My detractors accuse me of many things, but ostentatiousness is not one of them." He sounded proud. "A simple deployment of my device—the real one, not this early attempt—in the right place, at the right time, and it will all be over before you know it."

"Where is the device?"

Grubb tapped the side of his nose with his free hand. "I admit I am spilling information to you a little too freely, but that is a fact too far. I must have a soft spot for you, Hannah Chadwick. Even now, I seem convinced that I can persuade you to adopt our position."

"You can't."

"That's fine. But, I'll be keeping you under lock and key until it's done. Once you see the results, I'm sure your LineFolk side will come to the fore." Grubb gestured for her to take a step backward. "There have been a few hiccups in the plan, but your friend's resurrection has got us back on track. Thank you for waltzing in here a few days ago and just casually telling me that this selkie had survived her injuries. Our *help* on the lines is now a lot more motivated to provide assistance. The moment I sensed you both arrive tonight, I knew the time was nigh. And the time is now. Plans are in place for first light."

"What's Ruadh got to do with it?" Hannah was losing track.

"Enough. Remember the strongroom that I use as a transformation space for my patients? I think it will be ideal for keeping you both safe and sound until tomorrow. Please make your way through the door." Grubb nodded behind her and started to shuffle Ruadh forward. "If you go nicely, I won't harm the selkie."

Ruadh's eyes were wide and a little desperate. Hannah considered a variety of moves, but admitted to herself that all of them probably ended with the selkie being seriously hurt, or worse. She backed off, hands in the air, stepping slowly until she was in the huge doorframe that made up the no-go area. When Grubb was within a couple of metres, he stopped. "All the way in, please."

Hannah complied, walking backward until she touched the far wall. It didn't take long. The room was three metres square at most. Grubb roughly pushed Ruadh, and she stumbled in as well. He groaned as he attempted to push the steel door shut. It was a slow enough process that Ruadh clearly thought there was an opportunity, and she leapt forward, but Hannah grabbed her arm and stopped her.

"Not now."

A sheen of sweat broke out on Grubb's forehead. For a moment, he aged. His features returned from haemovore to human, and there wasn't a single extra wrinkle, but his face looked suddenly much older, as though his muscles redirected their energy to shutting the door and not to maintaining his perfect cheek structure. And then Hannah noticed what else redirected... his attention. For the moment, it was all on his effort to close the door.

Hannah leaned into Ruadh's ear, her mouth just a centimetre from the selkie's red hair. "We need to keep him contained until I can get to Baker Street. Get hold of the police. Maybe we'll be able to stop this."

Grubb was still having trouble. The door had shifted a few inches, but he clearly wasn't used to closing it, despite his bravado about using it as a strongroom.

"How?" Ruadh whispered. "We had our chance to rush him, and you stopped me."

The door moved a fraction more. Grubb's mouth split open wide again, and he snarled at them, in frustration at his failure to close it and as a warning to stay back. "Whispering does you no good."

He frowned suddenly, his snarl becoming an expression of confusion. He swatted the crown of his head as though a fly had landed there. Then he did the same on his arm. Then a third swipe on his lower back, and this time he left it there, making it look like something had hurt him.

There was a giggling sound.

"Who's there?" he growled, then snatched his remaining hand away from the door and looked at it. "Who touched me?"

The giggling got louder, and a cloud of dust kicked up from the floor in the strongroom. His eyes followed it as it moved around the small space, stopping in front of Hannah and Ruadh.

"Are you doing this?" he asked, taking a step into the room, but clearly reluctant to go much further. Suddenly, the giggling was joined by a chorus of chants, shouts, howls, and general merriment. Grubb jerked violently on the spot. It was as though he was under the control of a voodoo doll that was being stabbed with needles, and he lost his composure.

"Who's there?" he cried, even as his head snapped back and forth. It wasn't that he was being hit hard, just that the amount of pinches, prods, and tickles was too much to bear at once. He fell to his knees, and his haemovore features reasserted themselves.

"Now!" Hannah shouted, and they ran on either side of Grubb towards the door. But he still had enough fight in him to reach out his fingertips and grab Ruadh's ankle as she passed. The selkie collapsed to the ground next to him and kicked at his hand with her unrestrained foot. He seemed to find it easier to withstand this than whatever was invisibly assaulting him, but his transformation began to assert itself, and he both shrank and sprouted downy fur.

Hannah stopped in the doorway and looked back.

"Do it," Ruadh shouted. "While you can."

Hannah ran through the options in her head. Stop to help, and Grubb might get control again. Shut the door now, and Ruadh was trapped with the vampire. How quickly would he turn fully into a bat? Surely she could defend herself from a mouse with wings?

"I said do it," Ruadh insisted, and Hannah pushed. It was every bit as hard as Grubb had made it look and barely shifted.

"I'll try an' help, ma'am," said a voice in her ear. "Those who aren't teasing that man will do as well."

Nothing happened.

"Me too," called another voice. Then another, and another.

It wasn't much extra force, but it was enough. The door began to swing. Grubb realised what was happening and released Ruadh to get to his feet, but it was too late.

The door slammed with a deep metallic thump, and Hannah spun the handle as quickly as she could. Grubb hammered on the other side with his fists, but it was so thick, and he was shrinking so quickly, that there were only quiet taps from the other side.

Tap, tap, tap.

Hannah breathed with her forehead against the metal. Her breath condensed on the grey paint.

"Thank you, John," she said.

"It was our pleasures, ma'am. I was thinking about what you said. Time comes when we have to make a difference to what's going to happen. Not just knock about it. We can't do much, but if we all work together, then we can change things. Who knew that all that teasing young Pip does would give us the idea? An' we will keep teasing him until he leaves that lady with the red hair alone."

"You did change things. You've given me a chance. How did you know I was here and that we would need help?"

"'I'm not sure, but I feel like we are bound to these tunnels in a way that we ne'er were even at old Saltilack. We've been here longer than we were down there, after all. Maybe this is our home for good now. I think that means we can sense everything here."

"I'm glad," Hannah said, pulling her head from the door as Grubb's tapping was becoming annoying. She turned to the apparently empty room. "Is it still going to happen?"

"Yes, ma'am. Later today. In fact, very soon."

"But the Tube won't start up for hours," Hannah protested. "It makes no sense unless there are lots of people to hurt." She looked at her watch. "Oh."

It was five am. Somehow the night had passed. A faint vibration under her feet suggested that the first trains of the morning were running.

"Shit, I need to find help. Then get to Baker Street." She pulled out her phone. No signal at all, so she couldn't call Patel. What about Flynn? He never used a mobile, and Mia certainly wouldn't have hers on at this time of day. She would have to get above ground to call the police and then work out a different approach for getting to Flynn. Maybe a taxi. Which way was quicker? Back to the shop entrances in Notting Hill, or to clamber across the Circle Line? She didn't fancy the latter, particularly as she could hear a passing train.

"Will I...er...see you again, John?" she asked.

"If you spend long enough in the tunnels, and if there's a reason for us to knock for you, then why not?"

"John Puddle, I could kiss you."

She was as convinced as she could be that she would sense a blush, but the knocker said nothing more. The sound of giggling echoed from the tracks.

"Right, Han. To the surface."

She retraced steps back to the passageway. As she reached the door to the street, she heard a shrill bell ring. It was familiar. For a moment she thought it was the door, then she remembered it was similar to the sound that had drawn Flynn to the roof and to his marvellous parakeets.

Did Grubb use the same system? Of course! Why wouldn't he?

The bell rang again, and she turned back to the junction to see it vibrating at eye-level, attached to a wire running into the wall. There was a door next to it, and it seemed as good as any other option for what the source might be.

She stepped through, and there was a staircase, not dissimilar to the one hidden at number fifty, switching back on itself as it climbed several stories. It gave Hannah an idea.

She jogged up the stairs, arriving in a state of near exhaustion by a door at the top. She opened it to the roof, where the sun was trying to peek over the tops of the nearby buildings, and a moon hung low in the sky, looking three times its normal size.

She looked around and saw it a few metres away, nestled between two ventilation ducts. A green parakeet sitting on a perch. It spotted her and held out its foot.

"Sorry, bird," Hannah said. "I don't care what message you've brought." She unclipped the ring from its ankle and pulled out the paper, written in the Ogham script that she had seen at the clynic. She flipped it over and was relieved to see it was blank.

"Pen, pen, ah, pen," she muttered, spotting a pencil conveniently attached to a string so it couldn't stray far from the perch. She wrote a plea in English.

Grubb is releasing the gas NOW!

Come to Baker Street. NOW!

Then, for good measure, she added another **NOW!**

"God, if he doesn't get the message from this, he never will." She rolled the paper up, placed it back into the ring, and then onto the parakeet's foot. The address book was also attached by a string. Grubb was nothing if not cautious about losing things. She flicked through to the simplest of codes, a blacked-out square in the middle of the nine, and showed it to the bird.

"And ring like hell when you get there," she instructed it, having no idea whether it would understand. It took to the air immediately and flew to the west, where she hoped Flynn would be waking for his house visits. She watched the parakeet soar into a sun rising on what might be a very dark day for London.

Chapter 20

"WHERE ARE YOU, SHIV? Answer the fucking phone," Hannah pleaded just as the call connected.

Patel caught the tail end. "Consider my fucking phone answered," he laughed. "Someone got out of bed on the wrong side this morning."

"Shiv, shut up and listen to me. This is serious."

Although she couldn't see him, she sensed a change in his posture.

"Where are you?"

"I'm waiting for a Tube at Edgware Road. I'm trying to get to Baker Street." She was aware that her voice was shrill.

"I thought we spoke about this before. I really can't become a taxi service. You could buy a car."

"I don't need a lift," she shouted. "I need you, and however many police, army, whatever, that you can find, to stop him."

"Stop who?"

"Grubb, he's doing it. Now. He's going to kill everyone."

Patel said nothing for a while. "Shiv?" Hannah called. "Are you still there?"

"Yes, I'm here," he replied calmly. "I'm already there. Baker Street. Aditi is getting a tube down from her mother's at the crack of dawn.

I'm picking her up in ten minutes and taking her to school. She just messaged to say she's left Queens Park."

"Oh God, Shiv. Tell her to get off the train. She mustn't go as far as Baker Street."

"Why not, Hannah? What's going to happen?" He was still so calm. She couldn't believe it.

"Gas. He's releasing a gas into the tunnels. From the chamber where we met John. Can you stop the trains and clear the station?"

She could hear a tinny announcement in the background. He was already somewhere inside.

"You've no idea what you are asking. Clearing a station. Shutting down lines. That's the stuff we would do for a terrorist threat."

"What does this sound like?" Hannah screamed, aware that all around her, bleary-eyed passengers were staring. "Please, do whatever you can. I hope Flynn, Mia, and whoever else they rustle up are on their way to you now, assuming I worked the birds right. They can help. Get them into the station and into the chamber."

"Worked the birds..? Hannah, what are you on about?"

"Messenger birds. Parakeets. Oh, it's not important, but hopefully they summoned Flynn. He might know how to stop the gas."

"What does it do?"

"Does it matter? It's not good."

"It matters if I try to close a major London hub because someone sets off nothing more than a stink bomb."

"It's not a stink bomb. It's from Grubb's potion book. Something that's not from our biochemistry. It's from his world, but it kills people in ours. They're going to disperse it from the chamber through the ventilation shaft. Into the Jubilee line platforms, but it will spread to the Bakerloo from there."

"Bastard," Patel whispered.

"Does that mean you'll do it?"

"Alright, I'll try."

"Look out for Axton."

"Yeah." He cut the connection, and Hannah was suddenly helpless to do any more. She realised that he hadn't said he was going to warn his daughter to get off the Bakerloo line before she reached Baker Street.

She looked desperately at the arrivals board. The next train was in less than a minute. She stared into the mouth of the cut-and-cover tunnel, willing it to arrive. When it did, it was mercifully empty for this time of the morning. She stepped on before the doors had even finished opening and clung to the nearest handrail, her back to the carriage, looking purposefully out of the window. Every second in the station felt like a lifetime.

"C'mon, c'mon," she muttered, jigging up and down on the spot.

The familiar beeps were the precursor to the doors shutting, momentarily creating a cocoon of near silence before the train whined its way up to speed. Just two minutes later they pulled into the vaulted brick roof of the Circle Line platforms at Baker Street, the oldest underground railway station in the world. Hannah was virtually pressing her face to the glass. The doors didn't open. Why weren't they opening?

A bored announcement came over the tannoy from the driver.

"Sorry for the delay in activating the doors, ladies and gentlemen. We've been instructed to hold on platform for a while first. Not sure why, but I'm confident we'll be able to let you off shortly."

Hannah looked frantically left and right. She could see station staff hurriedly directing passengers off the platform. They were evacuating.

"Oh, Shiv, no. Not the Circle Line." She had told him the Jubilee and mentioned the Bakerloo, but they were emptying the Circle Line. It was much closer to the surface. The gas would be in the deeper tunnels. Maybe he had just issued a blanket evacuation order.

The driver came back on the tannoy. "As some of you have probably noticed, the platform is being emptied and we won't be able to let you off here. We'll continue on to Great Portland Street and, all being well, you can de-train there."

"No, no!" Hannah shouted and banged on the glass. A passing member of station staff glared at her and pointed east down the tunnel, shaking her head. "No, you don't understand. I have to get off here."

"Yeah, you and the rest of us," muttered someone from a few yards away in the carriage. "It's not all about you."

She ignored him and continued banging on the glass. Then she spotted the red emergency button and slammed her palm onto it.

"Oh, great," shouted the mutterer. "Now, we'll be stuck here until they've worked out you're a thoughtless cow."

"Yes?" said a voice from a speaker by the alarm. She assumed it was the driver.

"I need to get off here."

"Didn't you hear the announcement? The station is being evacuated. I'm waiting for a green light, and then we are moving on. No one is getting off."

"I *have* to get off here," she insisted. "I'm the reason for the evacuation."

There was silence in the carriage, and Hannah could sense a few people backing away towards the wide passageway that connected to the next. The driver was equally quiet.

"No, I mean I called it in. My name is Detective Sergeant Shiv Patel from the British Transport Police, and I have to get off."

"What carriage are you in?" the driver asked.

"I don't know," she admitted. "About halfway back."

"Are you sure you're BTP? Above the door. A letter."

"D."

"OK, I'm opening doors in D now, but only for a few seconds."

The beeps returned, and the doors slid open. Hannah didn't waste any time running out and up the platform towards the exit. It was nearly empty, with just a couple of shocked station staff watching her sprint towards them.

"What's the quickest way to the Jubilee Line platforms?" she wheezed as she approached.

"No one is going down to the Jubilee. You'll have to go straight to the surface, please," said the one who had shaken her head a moment ago.

Hannah ignored her and headed for the steps up to the station concourse. Baker Street was a bit of a warren, but the signs would send her in the right direction. The ticket hall was a seething mass of humanity, most of it trying to get up the staircases to the dim light of morning. Londoners seemed to just be getting on with it, and the staff were facilitating the evacuation with practiced ease.

"Shiv!" Hannah shouted. "Shiv!"

She heard a call over the hubbub. "Hannah! By the ticket machines."

She was on the other side of the barriers. They had all been opened to encourage a swift exit, and there were no queues. She ran through and saw Patel on her left, standing in conversation with a man in a blue tabard who was pressing a radio to the corner of his mouth.

"Did you call Aditi?" she gasped as she approached.

Patel held up a palm to the staff member to excuse himself momentarily. "Yeah, I mean no. I couldn't get her. She must be underground already."

"Are they holding the trains? The Circle Line is stopping, I think."

"Not yet. The deep lines take longer to coordinate." He ran a hand through his hair. "Look, are you sure about this? It's chaos. If it turns out there aren't good grounds for shutting down the station, my bollocks will be in my boss's fist, quick as you like, and she won't let go before I give her my resignation."

"I'm certain," Hannah insisted. "It's happening now. It might have already happened."

"Is this her?" blue tabard man interrupted. "The intelligence officer?" He looked Hannah up and down, taking in her flustered appearance. "You had bloody well better be right about this. We're shutting down the station just as rush hour is getting started. That's thousands of pissed-off commuters, and who are they going to complain to? Not you, that's for sure."

"Back off, Bill," Patel said, stepping in front of Hannah. "This is on me; my call."

"Yeah, well, if it were mine, we wouldn't be doing it. You can't even tell me what the actual threat is."

"Just get the platforms evacuated. We'll do the rest."

"Circle and Met lines are done. But the Jubilee and Bakerloo take longer. More pinch points for passengers." His radio crackled, and he held it to his ear for a moment. "There's a train in the southbound Jubilee platform, and then we are holding at Green Park, so that will be all clear once we get it out. The Bakerloo is more of a problem. There are two trains sitting in the tunnel to the north. We have to run them through, or the passengers are going to be pissed off. We'll de-train them at Oxford Circus."

"No," Patel said, "you have to hold them where they are."

"I can do that for fifteen minutes max, then they'll be running through. I thought the threat was focussed on the Jubilee platforms?"

"It is, we think," Hannah interjected.

"Think? We have downgraded confidence to 'think' now?" Tabard-man shook his head sadly.

Hannah turned to Patel. "We should get down to the chamber. Maybe we can stop the release?"

"I'll call for bomb disposal."

"This isn't a bomb, and it's like nothing you or they will have seen before."

"Then what can *we* do? I'm just a guy, and you are...whatever you are." For a moment, a flash of annoyance crossed Patel's face, and it rankled her..

"Hannah!" A call drifted across the ticket hall. "I got it! I got your message!"

Flynn and Mia hurried down the steps from the street. Pascal trailed behind them, tripping over his feet as though he wasn't used to his human form.

Hannah couldn't help herself. She ran into Flynn's surprised arms. "Thank God you're here."

"Your god has nothing to do with it," he insisted. "Are there LineFolk casualties?"

"LineFolk cas...? No, not sure yet. But that's not why I'm glad you're here. We need to stop Grubb's device activating, or if it already has, then contain it somehow."

"I don't know anything about it. How can I prevent it?"

"You worked it out at the top of the tower, so you'll work it out again."

"The Master worked it out. Not me."

"You *are* the Master now, Axton. You just have to start believing it."

Mia slid an arm through Flynn's. "She's right, Ax. You still think of yourself as an apprentice abclynician, but you are so much more than that. You carry a thousand years of LineFolk wisdom. This is your time."

"It came too early, Mi. You remember what Julius said. I'm not ready."

"You are as ready as the lunatic who has created this scheme to kill so many dwellers."

"Don't refer to my brother as a lunatic."

Mia removed her arm. "Brother?"

"Yes. Maybe. I don't know," he huffed, clearly exasperated. "I'm so confused. I feel a connection to a man whom my logical brain detests. I remember happy times—entire lifetimes when we were inseparable."

Hannah caught Mia's eye and held it. "He's not turning into Wayworthy. He just has his memories."

Mia seemed to be considering this and taking a moment to accept it, when she was knocked flying by a commuter hurrying to the exits. She fell to her knees, and Hannah saw her flex her fingers as though extending invisible claws, ready to strike in revenge. Emotions warring within her, Mia quickly regained control, and when Flynn helped her to her feet, her features were calm.

Patel's were not. "If you lot are going to do something, now might be a great time to do it."

"Shiv's right," Hannah said. "We should go to the chamber where I met John Puddle and see what we're dealing with."

She led the group back through the barriers, where Patel showed ID to allow them passage against the flow of humanity from below.

"Can you find the way?" he asked. "I want to stay up here and see if I can find out where Aditi's train is."

Hannah nodded and ran towards the Jubilee Line escalators. Flynn and Mia kept up easily, even when she sped down the moving staircase two steps at a time, always on the point of tripping, but Pascal was stymied by it and stood at the top, putting a toe onto the metal and pulling it back in horror. The others didn't notice, and when they reached the bottom, the ogre was still pacing in frustration on the landing.

Hannah pointed. "Look!" There was a male figure lying on the ground. He was wearing an orange tabard, and a radio sat in his limp fingers, squawking with the panicked communication flowing around the station staff.

"Has he tripped?" Mia asked. There was nothing for him to fall over. He was sprawled face down on the dirty concrete floor, yards from any obstructions.

Hannah ground to a halt and held her arms out to stop the others. "Oh, no." She closed her eyes and whispered, "Stay behind me. I don't know if it's going to hurt you as well."

"What is?" Flynn asked, trying to push past, but Hannah was immovable. "I know I'm not a human doctor, but I can check the basics."

Hannah's arms were rigid. "I said, stay back. I think this is Grubb's first victim, and probably not his last. In fact, the next might be us if the gas is spreading in this direction."

She focussed her mind on the linether that surrounded them so close to the Ouroborus. It was dense here; there was no suggestion that its supply was limited. Hannah let it play with her senses, swirling around her as though she were the centre of a wormhole. Then she extended her reach towards the prone figure on the floor, and as she did, the nature of the linether changed. It stopped being pure. It became sullied. Every molecule, electron, wave—she had no idea what it actually was and there probably wasn't an English word for it anyway—had a partner, and that partner meant death.

"I can feel it," she said simply. "It's dangerous, but not poisonous. It wants to make us hate."

"Us? Is it trying to reach us?" Mia asked, backing off slightly.

"Not consciously, but this is a magical creation for one purpose only, and it feels lost without fulfilling that."

There was a wail from behind them. Hannah had forgotten about Pascal, and as she snapped her head round at the sound, she saw the ogre tumbling down the central barrier between the up and down escalators, completely out of control as he bounced over warning signs. He had obviously decided to avoid using the stairs themselves.

In a second he was on them and crashed into Mia and Flynn, who consequently took Hannah with them three metres deeper into the concourse. Pascal landed on Mia's back, and she snarled with the pressure on her still-healing wounds.

"Sorry, sorry," he muttered. "I sorry."

Hannah looked up from the floor. She couldn't see it with her eyes, but the LineFolk part of her could feel it coming, only feet away from where they lay.

"No," she commanded and reached out to the compromised linether with all her might, praying that whatever was attached to it would let it respond to her power. It didn't at first. It had fuzzy edges and resisted her mental grip, but gradually she wrestled it under control, balancing it between the magical influence that normally allowed linether to move and the more mortal gaseous mechanics that were drifting it towards them. She realised she could feel a breeze from the platforms and that she was competing with it. Trains were still moving on the deep lines.

Hannah pushed the linether back, creating something akin to a vacuum of elemental power in front of them. She felt the miasma move with it. Mia gasped. "Hannah, I can sense the transformation coming. What are you doing?"

"Shit," Hannah muttered. "Of course. I can't push it all away, or you'll transform." She relaxed, and the contamination began to drift back towards them.

"Maybe we should just change?" Flynn suggested. "Who knows what we'll find down there."

"Pascal won't fit through some of these tunnels. I think I can separate the contaminated linether from the good stuff." Hannah concentrated on the feel of the linether that was enveloped by the miasma.

With painstaking control that surprised her, she made it retreat to the edges of the chamber where it was poised in the entranceways. She prayed that there was no one new entering from the platforms.

Flynn and Mia untangled themselves from Pascal. "I think it's clear," Hannah told them, "at least, I hope it is."

"We are placing a lot of faith in hope," Flynn stated.

"Don't we always? I pushed the miasma back to the edges. It took some linether with it, but I'm keeping an envelope near us."

Flynn looked at her, then into the chamber. "OK, I trust you." He strode purposefully towards the figure on the floor, as though leaping into action before he could change his mind. Mia went to follow, but Hannah held her back.

"There's no point in you taking the risk as well. If Flynn is OK, you will be. I'm not in the same position. Maybe I'm too human."

Flynn knelt by the man and placed two fingers on his neck. He waited for a few moments, then shook his head. "Very dead, unless genuine humans have arteries in different places." He bent lower to peer at the man's face. "And he has a look of pure terror, or maybe anger. What did he see?"

"He didn't see anything," Hannah replied. "He hated himself to death."

"On the spot?"

"On the spot. That's what Grubb told me would happen to dwellers."

"Can you tell if there are others deeper in the station?"

"No, so we need to find the source. I think I can create a bubble to keep us safe. Really, to keep me safe. I suspect you are OK."

"My brother never liked therians. If there is one type of LineFolk he would have neglected to exclude, it's Mia and me."

"Noted." With the four of them standing next to the body, Hannah relaxed her grip on the contaminated linether enough to let it, and whatever was leeching off it, surround them at a distance of five yards on all sides. This felt like a comfortable balance between space and the effort required. "Hold on to my arms, my back, my waist. Just don't step away from me."

She tried to get her bearings. All London Tube stations had a habit of looking the same when you were thirty metres under the city streets, and she was mainly familiar with the Bakerloo line. The chamber where they had met John Puddle was next to the Jubilee. She followed her nose and the more useful signs deeper into the station. As they travelled, two more bodies showed themselves, both clearly employees. They had done a heroic job of evacuating passengers and had paid the ultimate price.

Their eyes on the bodies rather than the floor, there was some tripping over each other, and particularly the gobsmacked Pascal, as they tried to stay close.

"Why is he here?" Hannah asked, looking at the ogre.

"He followed us," Mia shrugged. "Trundle is babysitting."

"That's one hell of a redemption arc," Hannah scoffed. "I wish her no harm, but only a few weeks ago she was hoping for evidence of my horrible death at the hands of Tafs. Now you are leaving the kittens with her?"

"She's never done anything to hurt Ax and me, or the kids. Even Tafs loved them in her own way."

Hannah tried to ignore her trust issues. "We're here." She looked at the simple door to the baffle chamber. "If John was right, this is ground zero. It's in here."

"It's also locked," Flynn said, observing the lack of a handle and a single keyhole.

"It didn't stop Shiv. He just..." Hannah mimed a shoulder-charge.

"Before any of us are stupid enough to try that," Mia interjected. "What can you sense on the other side?"

"What you would expect. The miasma is there; in fact, it's concentrated, but it's also shifting. There is a lot of moving air. I see why Grubb chose this spot. The ventilation shaft and the baffle mean that there's a gale blowing."

"But you can make it safe?"

"I think I'll be able to get us in there. But should we approach it? I don't know. If it's kicking out the miasma as fast as I can disperse it, then we're stuffed."

"More hope over logic then?"

"It's becoming our thing," Hannah smiled.

"Then let's do it." Mia suddenly charged at the door. Hannah had forgotten how strong she was. It didn't just gently pop ajar as it had when Patel tried, but smashed open with a crash that threatened to take it off its hinges.

There was a man sitting cross-legged at the entrance to the baffle alcove. He was alive, but had his head in his hands and barely looked up when the door opened.

"You!" Hannah said. "You were here last week. You threw us out."

"I didn't want to turn the machine on," he sobbed. "I had no choice. Once I knew she hadn't died, he had control over me again."

"You are unharmed. You're LineFolk," Hannah pointed out.

"In a fashion, yes."

"You're LineFolk and you work on the lines."

He looked up at Hannah and nodded gently.

"You are Ruadh's father."

Chapter 21

THE MAN'S FACE IMMEDIATELY lit up. "Do you know her? Have you seen her?"

"Yes," Hannah replied. "We've seen her. I was with her until recently."

"Then this was worth it," he said with a tormented expression. "He'll release us now."

Hannah didn't want to tell him that Ruadh was currently locked in a room with Grubb, or that Mia was Tarrin's daughter. She pointed at the box sitting on the ground next to him.

"Is that what I think it is?"

He turned his head slowly, as though not wanting to admit it was there. "Yes. It's empty now. The wind took it all." Tears ran down his face. "How many?"

"Dead? Not as many as you probably hope. Small blessing. We managed to evacuate the station in time. But some of the staff were killed in doing so."

"No, no!" the selkie sobbed. Hannah thought he might be mourning the death of colleagues and maybe friends, but instead he was mourning the failure. "He'll make me do it all over again."

"We won't let you," Mia said firmly. "Nothing is worth this much death."

His face said otherwise. "If not me, then he'll get to someone else. He has that power over the lines. I was just a useful idiot who knew about the baffles and how well it would work if we released it here. It's quiet too. No one comes here except me."

The breeze picked up, and his fringe danced in the wind. It was drawn away from the platform towards the ventilation shaft.

"I thought you said the station was evacuated?" he asked. "So why are trains still running?"

"We haven't managed to shut all the lines down yet. Just the subsurface ones."

"I haven't seen a train come in on the Jubilee for ten minutes now." His face brightened. "It must be the Bakerloo. It's active. Maybe there's still a chance!"

"Do you mean a chance of enough people dying?"

He looked ashamed. "Yes, and that we'll be free to go back to the sea."

"Aditi!" Hannah exclaimed. "Shiv's daughter. She's on a southbound Bakerloo right now. This might be her train!"

"Can you clear the gas from the platform?" Flynn asked.

"No, not all of it. I'm getting tired, and these few metres are about my limit."

"Then we need to prevent it from entering the station somehow."

"I don't see how. We can't change the signals," Hannah stated. She looked at the selkie.

"How much do you know about this gas, the miasma? Will the carriages be airtight enough to stop it?"

"Not for long. There's nothing you can do. If the train stops on the platform for as little as two minutes, it will leak in. If they open the doors as well, then it's as good as over." He smiled, and Hannah sensed he was already plotting his route back to Scotland with Ruadh.

"Your daughter made the right choices. I suggest that you take this chance to do the same." Hannah pulled Flynn toward the door. "Let's get to the platform and work out what to do."

At a run, it only took them half a minute to reach the southbound Bakerloo Line. The breeze intensified, and Hannah struggled to split her concentration between keeping the miasma at bay and heading in the right direction. Flynn, Mia, and Pascal stuck close, in case Grubb had only protected anthrothropes. She wasn't sure if she counted as that.

They reached the platform to hear the tracks rattling and an otherworldly screech of an incoming train. Hannah headed for the far end, and as it came in, she stood in full view of the driver, waving her arms frantically. "Don't open the doors," she shouted. "Keep them shut. Move straight out."

Hannah glanced at the signal at the tunnel entrance. Red. She thought the last remaining trains were running through, but there must be a jam in the tunnels ahead.

The driver was a young woman. She looked at the frantic Hannah and cocked her head.

"Keep them closed!" Hannah screamed again, not sure if the instruction from the control centre to hold passengers on the train had got through.

The driver gave the appearance of wishing she hadn't been rostered that morning. She reached for her radio. Surely she would receive the message now?

"They're sitting here too long," Hannah muttered. "It might be leaking in already." She could sense the miasma exploring the gaps between the doors and the vents above the windows.

"How can we get her to leave?" Mia asked. "I've heard of emergency stop, but never emergency start. I would push it if I could."

Hannah looked at her in astonishment. "Of course *you* can't. You're strong, but not that strong. But I know a man who can!" She shifted her gaze to Pascal, who was standing wide-eyed next to an advert on the wall for a West End musical.

"He's in human form, darling. He's a weakling like that."

Hannah steeled herself. "I'll change him. I know I can. I'll stop the linether from disguising him." She paused. "But I can't do that *and* hold back the miasma."

They all knew what that meant. They would be placing all their faith in Grubb's not wanting to risk harming LineFolk. And Hannah herself would be taking the biggest gamble of all.

She looked at Pascal. "I'm able to make you change to your true form. If I do, are you strong enough to push the train out of the station?"

It seemed as though he didn't understand because he leaned forward, cocking an ear to the group. "Sorry. Slower, please."

"If you are an ogre," Hannah mimed an inflated, muscly stance, "can you push the train?"

He adopted the most French expression of disgust Hannah had ever seen. This was clearly an insulting question. "*For sure*, I can push the train."

"Come on then," she pulled him down the platform towards the rear. "Flynn, Mia, don't let her open the doors. I'll see you again in a minute. I hope."

It took thirty seconds to reach the other end, during which the carriages stayed shut, but the train remained stationary. When they reached the back, she peered down the platform. Flynn and Mia were still standing, with the female werecat adopting a stance that was borderline aggressive. It would certainly encourage the driver to keep the doors locked.

"Are you ready?" she said to Pascal.

"Yes," he replied.

"Don't you mean, oui?" She tried to lighten the mood.

"I am speaking English, so why I say oui?"

"OK, there's no time for jokes I can tell. I'm going to push the linether away from you. That means your true form will come back. Probably suddenly."

Pascal turned his back on her, calmly removed his clothes, and sat on the platform cross-legged. She took that as a sign that he was prepared.

Hannah realised that she didn't need to close her eyes any longer to sense the linether. It was just there, like a veil over the real world, and very busy in front of her, powering Pascal's disguise. It hit her that the changes were almost completely involuntary, which made the linether slightly abusive in its pursuit of hiding the LineFolk. A question for Flynn, on another day, if another day came for her.

The linether teased her by concentrating around Pascal as though it knew what she was about to do, then with a single thought she dispersed it in all directions. The ogre must have felt its absence immediately, as a startled expression dropped onto his face.

"Putain!" he gasped, dropping into French, despite his protestations.

His head changed first, expanding comically to three-times its human size. His neck muscles clearly had trouble supporting it, because it lolled to the left, and he fixed Hannah with a sideways glare that made a mockery of his consent. Then his torso caught up, and a muscular form expanded outwards. Hannah noted that this was far more refined and controlled than other transformations she had been close to, and nothing like the skin-splitting, organ-remodelling that the cyoeraeths had endured. This was more of a proportionate growth of the human shape, only without the arms and legs having been informed. It occurred to Hannah that Patel was going to have a fine time scrubbing the CCTV footage after today's events; there was no justifying *this* as AI. Within twenty seconds, the transformation was complete, and Pascal panted, in gigantic ogre form, in front of her. A face was pressed against the glass of the rear carriage, a woman with a coat over her scrubs, mouth agape in shock. A nurse like Hannah. It was the only dweller to have seen the change, and maybe the only one that Patel would need to persuade into silence.

"There are four lines. Can you see where the wheels run? Those are fine to tread on, but not the others. Electricity. Boom. Pascal dead."

He didn't reply, not even with a nod, but stepped carefully into the tracks, placing his feet on either side of the safety pit in the middle. The train must weigh two hundred tonnes. How could he possibly move it? But move it, he did. He placed a broad shoulder against the back of the car and pushed. It was all the more impressive because the brakes were on and the wheels screeched in protest as they were forced along the rails. Ten metres, twenty, and he achieved some momentum. This situation registered back in the cab, because the brakes disengaged with a sharp hiss and the motion became smoother, then accelerated as the driver pulled the train out of the station, despite the red light. Pascal found himself jogging to keep up, then finally stopped pushing and watched as the train disappeared into the southbound tunnel. It travelled several hundred metres before they heard it decelerate again, the driver deciding that she had reached a point of safety far enough away from whatever was pushing her train, but not getting so close to the one in front.

"Pascal, you're a hero," Hannah said, catching up with him. "And we're alive!" She paused and realised she had been holding her breath, then let it go and refilled her lungs.

Still alive. No feelings of impending rage.

They had done it.

***

Hannah had asked Pascal if he wanted to remain as an ogre for a while, just in case another train came in, and he was happy to, but there wasn't a whisper of moving air on the platform once the southbound train had gone. The line was shut. She let him stay huge for a while as it took a lot less effort to maintain the exclusion zone for the linether than it did to create it in the first place.

She found an emergency communication console and stabbed the blue button to speak to someone in station control.

"Keep everyone away," she said. "The Bakerloo is clear, but there's still a threat if anyone comes down."

"Hannah?" asked a tinny voice over the intercom that she recognised. "It's me, Shiv. Aditi?"

"Not here. She's either on a train outside, or on the one that Pascal just pushed out. Whatever, she's safe."

"Oh God, thank you. I'll try to call her now."

"She's still thirty metres under the ground, so don't panic if she doesn't pick up. Just give her time."

The connection went dead for a moment, then a new voice came online. "This is Chief Superintendent Fishbourne. Am I speaking to Hannah Chadwick?"

"Yes," Hannah replied quietly, unsure of what was going to happen.

"We've only got your word for it that there was something to worry about in the first place, and similarly, that everyone is now safe."

"Not everyone. There are at least three bodies down here."

"I see. You seem to have a habit of being in the right spot at the right time for events that threaten the city."

"What are you saying?" Hannah asked, taking a mild dislike to the policewoman.

"I'll let DS Patel deal with you."

Hannah dropped the call and slumped to the ground. Mia and Flynn joined her.

"Learned anything surprising about yourself this time?" Flynn asked. "Any new secret powers?"

"Not that I noticed, just the gift of patience that gave me the restraint not to throw something at the wall after that conversation."

"That's the best gift of all. I wish I shared it."

"One of your personalities must have."

"You are always encouraging me to suppress them. Anyway, from what I've seen in my memories, I don't think calmness was a defining trait of my job in the past. The Master was the first abclynician to have zen-like self-control. Maybe the last."

"Is he here now?"

"Yes, a little closer than usual. He couldn't stay away from all this excitement."

"Is he proud of me?"

Flynn smiled. "Very."

Chapter 22

"No headache this time?" Patel asked as they sat down at a familiar table in the same Lebanese restaurant.

"No," Hannah smiled. "The headaches are gone for good. Knocker-generated ones, I mean."

"I'm glad we had a chance to do this again. I would have wanted to anyway, because I need to say sorry for the last time."

"For what?"

"For shutting the conversation down when you tried to ask me about Flora. I'm not promising to talk about her tonight; in fact, I'm telling you now that I won't, but every day you make me feel a little more open to the possibility."

Hannah took his hand across the table. "I know you have your reasons and I'm not going to ask again. You were just being...you."

"A grumpy idiot?"

"Yeah. You."

"I am, as they say, a product of my time and upbringing. I promise I'll change."

Hannah leaned into her chair. "God, I'm so tired. I slept like a log last night, and I'm still burned out. I don't know how you look so fresh." He really was—as though he'd uncovered a new passion for life. She found herself wondering if that passion was her. "I've spent days trying to track down Ruadh. There was a note through the letterbox at number fifty when we got back that afternoon. I think it was from her."

"What makes you say that?"

"It said, 'I fucking hate bats'."

"Nothing else?"

"Nope. I imagine that when Grubb's assistant turned up the next day, he let them out. She probably spent the night swatting a really irritated vampire bat away. I guess she ran. Grubb would have known that the plan had failed by then."

"And we couldn't find any record of the man you saw in the chamber, her father. We have a human name for him, of course, the one he was working under, but that draws a blank. He's getting paid into a bank account like everyone else, though, so we'll catch him at some point."

"Be kind when you do."

"He doesn't deserve it. He won't get human justice. We can't risk that. I'll work out another way to make him see the error of his ways."

"I don't like that, Shiv. When you find him, let me help."

Patel scowled, and for a moment she thought the date was about to go the same way as the first one, but he relaxed.

"It's been a busy few days, Han. The Chief has carried a lot, but you know she has to leave most of it to me. And it took a while to persuade my ex I wasn't being negligent by letting Aditi skip straight past Baker Street and miss a morning of school."

"Did she see anything on the platform? Anything she shouldn't, I mean."

Patel shook his head and savoured a long swig of wine. "No, just a woman, you I imagine, and a little guy running up and down, then a couple of others waving their arms frantically as the train left the station without letting her off. She thinks it's funny. I told her someone did a bad fart and that I'm now in the fart police."

Hannah laughed. "That sounds more appealing than what you actually do."

"Yeah, about that." He paused, and Hannah saw a look of concern flash across his face.

"What, Shiv?"

"I don't think I can do this any more. Not in the way I have been doing."

"I don't understand."

"I've spent years policing both worlds, trying to balance them. Making sense of it all so that others don't have to."

"And you do it brilliantly."

"I screw it up time and time again, Hannah, and you know it. If it weren't for you, Golden Square, Baker Street—they both would have been disasters. I got soft and thought I could let the two worlds co-exist. Well, that's not true."

"It has to be true."

"No." He looked her in the eyes, and for a moment she saw the light go out of his. "The freaks nearly killed Aditi. She's a little girl going to school, meeting her dad, and they nearly killed her. She was on her own. She would have died, terrified and on her own."

"Shiv, I'm sorry, but we stopped it."

"We shouldn't have had to. I'll never forgive them for that. Never."

"It was Grubb. You can't blame a whole people for one man's evil."

"Grubb, Tarrin, Tafs, Trundle, Dafyd. Where does it end? They're all the same, Hannah. They don't give a shit about us. And so I'm going to stop giving a shit about them."

She nibbled her lower lip, and Patel looked at the wall. Her hand was resting on the table, and she pushed it forward a centimetre, but he didn't take it back. She bit the bullet and reached across to grasp his. For a moment he shifted attention back to her, and he gave her fingers a light squeeze, then leaned away.

"I'll need your help, Hannah," he said. "To get them under control. It's now or never."

She said nothing. This was the biggest problem with different beings coexisting. Keeping the balance wasn't easy; there was a constant need for restraint, and it wasn't always on the part of the LineFolk.

***

The journey had been lengthy, and Pascal wasn't brilliant company. Hannah hadn't felt as though they could risk the train in case she couldn't keep control, so they drove in a horsebox van she rented from a depot near Folkestone. Pascal sat up front as long as she kept his human disguise intact, but he was ready to jump into the back if she sensed it slipping.

The effort required through the Channel Tunnel was immense, but she maintained his form. Soon after leaving Calais it became too much and the linether began to leak away from the cab. She pulled over in a dark corner of a French autoroute aire, and Pascal shuffled into the box, the truck suspension creaking under his weight as he clambered into the back.

He couldn't direct her precisely because he'd never left his home until he was taken a few weeks previously in the dead of the night, by men with nets, guns, and a lot of bravado.

Men.

They had to have been. There was no linether here and so no way of disguising. The ogre's kidnappers were humans. On this side of the Channel, there were people who knew about OtherFolk.

The forest road was dark, and Hannah leaned forward, peering through the gloom. The van's headlights were next to useless.

"Here, please," Pascal said suddenly, peering through a hatch into the cab. "Maybe here."

She stepped out of the cab and stretched after a day of travelling, then walked to the back and cracked the doors a little.

"Ready?" she asked.

"Yes."

She relaxed, Pascal smiled as best he could in ogre form, and climbed down, towering over her, as naked as the day he was born. Assuming ogres were born naked. He didn't touch her—his strength was enormous, and there was too much risk of hurting her by mistake. Instead, he put a hand where she thought his heart might be, and then made a deep bellowing roar that disappeared into the surrounding forest.

For a moment it was quiet, and then a faint howl came from the trees.

Pascal smiled, touched his chest again, and walked slowly into the woods. Within seconds, he was gone.

***

Axton Flynn was a frantic abclynician. Business had picked up very rapidly since the events at Baker Street station, and with Hannah absent with Pascal, he was back to playing abclynician, nurse, *and* receptionist. Mia had helped out occasionally, but she was not equipped with a bedside manner, and Flynn encouraged her to busy herself elsewhere.

When he finally closed the clynic door at the end of the day, he trudged up the stairs to the first floor. The smell of cooking meat wafted down from the upper storeys, and he licked his lips in anticipation of a hearty meal.

There was a draft on the landing. There had been ever since Pascal trashed the room. The bookcases wouldn't quite latch back into place, and every passing train blew a gust up the stairs and into the house. He was just about to attempt to fix that for the tenth time when the parakeet bell rang, and he excitedly ran to the roof past a bemused Mia. He still loved those birds.

There was a new arrival on the perch, most likely a request for a visit, but what caught his eye was the scrap of paper on the floor. It was wet from days of damp weather, and he had to peel it off with his fingernails. He had dropped it there on the morning of the events at Baker Street, and the rain had stuck it loosely to the lead roof.

Hannah's message was still distinct.

Grubb is releasing the gas NOW!

Come to Baker Street. NOW!

NOW!

Flynn smiled, but he hadn't been smiling at the time. He had been torn. Helping dwellers wasn't his problem, was it?

He flipped the sheet over, and his heart skipped. A message in ogham, one that presumably had been sent to Grubb's before Hannah reused the paper.

He read it once, then checked his translation. Then again, for good measure.

Chadwick isn't what we think she is. It's much worse.

Axton Flynn, abclynician of number fifty, werecat, master of the clynic, and legacy bearer of a thousand years of LineFolk wisdom, sat down on the damp roof and collected his thoughts. The truth was all there somewhere. He just had to find it.

THE END

The LineFolk Of London will return in Book Three: Unusual Afflictions

I hope you want to read more from the world of the LineFolk of London and continue following Hannah, Flynn, Mia, and Patel as they encounter more mythical beasts and insurmountable challenges.

UNUSUAL AFFLICTIONS

THE LINEFOLK OF LONDON: BOOK THREE

JAY NEILL

MID-2026

If you would like to be notified when Unusual Afflictions publishes in mid-2026, please join my community at:

www.jayneill.com/newsletter

Support me in writing more about the world of the LineFolk

I hope you enjoyed disappearing into the world of a hidden London.

You've already done the most important thing by reading this story, but there are other (free!) things you can do as well.

I would be ecstatic if you would leave a review wherever you like to drop your bookish thoughts. Reviews are so important for independent authors, and every one makes a difference. Amazon and Goodreads are the main spots, but you will know your favourite.

If you aren't yet a member of my reader community, you can join at www.jayneill.com. You can get access to advance reader programmes, sample chapters, and more.

About the author

Jay Neill is a British author of high-concept urban fantasy, specialising in the collision of the mundane and the magical. After 25 years in the corporate sector, he switched to writing fiction to build worlds hidden just beneath our reality.

His first novel, **The Terminus Of All Things**, is a standalone urban portal fantasy that explores the concept of Endland, a chaotic, mirror-dystopia built from the obsolete remnants of our own world.

Jay's new series is The LineFolk of London, a separate venture into British mythology where all UK mythological creatures are forced to live within the restricted boundaries of the London Underground's Circle Line, surviving only by harnessing a unique magical energy source: Linether.

Jay's witty, structured approach to modern fantasy has seen him compared to authors like Ben Aaronovitch (Rivers of London) for his use of real-world infrastructure and Robert Rankin for his eccentric, inventive British comedy and urban mythologising.

***

Connect with Jay

- TikTok – www.tiktok.com/@jay.neill5
- Instagram – www.instagram.com/jayneill.author
- Threads – www.threads.com/@jayneill.author
- BlueSky – bsky.app/profile/jayneill.com
- Facebook – www.facebook.com/jayneill.fantasyauthor
- Visit Jay's website www.jayneill.com to join his community and access bonus content, updates, advanced reader copy programmes and more.

Printed in Dunstable, United Kingdom

80924540R00129